ROYALTY-FREE ONE-ACT PLAYS

Edited by

J. CRABB

Black Box Press
Los Angeles

NOTE: All plays contained in this anthology are in the public domain and may, therefore, be performed without paying royalties.

ISBN 978-1-4303-2970-1

First Edition

CONTENTS

THE BOOR

Anton Chekhov

CHARACTERS:

HELENA IVANOVNA POPOV, *young widow, mistress of a country estate*
GRIGORI STEPANOVITCH SMIRNOV, *proprietor of a country estate*
LUKA, servant of MRS. POPOV
A gardener. A Coachman. Several workmen.

TIME: The present.

[A well-furnished reception-room in MRS. POPOV'S home. MRS. POPOV is discovered in deep mourning, sitting upon a sofa, gazing steadfastly at a photograph. LUKA is also present.]

LUKA: It isn't right, ma'am. You're wearing yourself out! The maid and the cook have gone looking for berries; everything that breathes is enjoying life; even the cat knows how to be happy--slips about the courtyard and catches birds--but you hide yourself here in the house as though you were in a cloister. Yes, truly, by actual reckoning you haven't left this house for a whole year.

MRS. POPOV: And I shall never leave it--why should I? My life is over. He lies in his grave, and I have buried myself within these four walls. We are both dead.

LUKA: There you are again! It's too awful to listen to, so it is! Nikolai Michailovitch is dead; it was the will of the Lord, and the Lord has given him eternal peace. You have grieved over it and that ought to be enough. Now it's time to stop. One can't weep and wear mourning forever! My wife died a few years ago. I grieved for her. I wept a whole month--and then it was over. Must one be forever singing lamentations? That would be more than your husband was worth! *[He sighs.]* You have forgotten all your neighbors. You don't go out and you receive no one. We live--you'll pardon me--like the spiders, and the good light of day we never see. All the livery is eaten by mice--as though there weren't any more nice people in the world! But the whole neighborhood is full of gentlefolk. The regiment is stationed in Riblov--officers--simply beautiful! One can't see enough of them! Every Friday a ball, and military music every day. Oh, my dear, dear ma'am, young and pretty as you are, if you'd only let your spirits live--! Beauty can't last forever. When ten short years are over, you'll be glad enough to go out a bit and meet the officers--and then it'll be too late.

MRS. POPOV: *[Resolutely.]* Please don't speak of these things again. You know very well that since the death of Nikolai Michailovitch my life is absolutely nothing to me. You think I live, but it only seems so. Do you understand? Oh, that his departed soul may see how I love him! I know, it's no secret to you; he was often unjust to me, cruel, and--he wasn't faithful, but I shall be faithful to the grave and prove to him how *I* can love. There, in the Beyond, he'll find me the same as I was until his death.

LUKA: What is the use of all these words, when you'd so much rather go walking in the garden or order Tobby or Welikan harnessed to the trap, and visit the neighbors?

MRS. POPOV: *[Weeping.]* Oh!

LUKA: Madam, dear madam, what is it? In Heaven's name!

MRS. POPOV: He loved Tobby so! He always drove him to the Kortschagins or the Vlassovs. What a wonderful horseman he was! How fine he looked when he pulled at the reigns with all his might! Tobby, Tobby--give him an extra measure of oats to-day!

LUKA: Yes, ma'am.

[A bell rings loudly.]

MRS. POPOV: *[Shudders.]* What's that? I am at home to no one.

LUKA: Yes, ma'am.

[He goes out, centre.]

MRS. POPOV: *[Gazing at the photograph.]* You shall see, Nikolai, how I can love and forgive! My love will die only with me--when my poor heart stops beating. *[She smiles through her tears.]* And aren't you ashamed? I have been a good, true wife; I have imprisoned myself and I shall remain true until death, and you--you--you're not ashamed of yourself, my dear monster! You quarreled with me, left me alone for weeks--

[LUKA enters in great excitement.]

LUKA: Oh, ma'am, someone is asking for you, insists on seeing you--

MRS. POPOV: You told him that since my husband's death I receive no one?

LUKA: I said so, but he won't listen; he says it is a pressing matter.

MRS. POPOV: I receive no one!

LUKA: I told him that, but he's a wild man; he swore and pushed himself into the room; he's in the dining-room now.

MRS. POPOV: *[Excitedly.]* Good. Show him in. The impudent--!

[LUKA goes out, centre.]

MRS. POPOV: What a bore people are! What can they want with me? Why do they disturb my peace? *[She sighs.]* Yes, it is clear I must enter a convent. *[Meditatively.]* Yes, a convent.

[SMIRNOV enters, followed by LUKA.]

SMIRNOV: *[To LUKA.]* Fool, you make too much noise! You're an ass! *[Discovering MRS. POPOV--politely.]* Madam, I have the honor to introduce myself: Lieutenant in the Artillery, retired, country gentleman, Grigori Stapanovitch Smirnov! I'm compelled to bother you about an exceedingly important matter.

MRS. POPOV: *[Without offering her hand.]* What is it you wish?

SMIRNOV: Your deceased husband, with whom I had the honor to be acquainted, left me two notes amounting to about twelve hundred roubles. Inasmuch as I have to pay the interest tomorrow on a loan from the Agrarian Bank, I should like to request, madam, that you pay me the money today.

MRS. POPOV: Twelve-hundred--and for what was my husband indebted to you?

SMIRNOV: He bought oats from me.

MRS. POPOV: *[With a sigh, to LUKA.]* Don't forget to give Tobby an extra measure of oats.

[LUKA goes out.]

MRS. POPOV: *[To SMIRNOV.]* If Nikolai Michailovitch is indebted to you, I shall, of course, pay you, but I am sorry, I haven't the money to-day. Tomorrow my manager will return from the city and I shall notify him to pay you what is due you, but until then I cannot satisfy your request. Furthermore, today is just seven months since the death of my husband, and I am not in the mood to discuss money matters.

SMIRNOV: And I am in the mood to fly up the chimney with my feet in the air if I can't lay hands on that interest tomorrow. They'll seize my estate!

MRS. POPOV: Day after tomorrow you will receive the money.

SMIRNOV: I don't need the money day after tomorrow; I need it today.

MRS. POPOV: I'm sorry I can't pay you today.

SMIRNOV: And I can't wait until day after tomorrow.

MRS. POPOV: But what can I do if I haven't it?

SMIRNOV: So you can't pay?

MRS. POPOV: I cannot.

SMIRNOV: Hm! Is that your last word?

MRS. POPOV: My last.

SMIRNOV: Absolutely?

MRS. POPOV: Absolutely.

SMIRNOV: Thank you. *[He shrugs his shoulders.]* And they expect me to stand for all that. The toll-gatherer just now met me in the road and asked why I was always worrying. Why, in Heaven's name, shouldn't I worry? I need money, I feel the knife at my throat. Yesterday morning I left my house in the early dawn and called on all my debtors. If even one of them had paid his debt! I worked the skin off my fingers! The devil knows in what sort of Jew-inn I slept; in a room with a barrel of brandy! And now at last I come here, seventy versts from home, hope for a little money, and all you give me is moods! Why shouldn't I worry?

MRS. POPOV: I thought I made it plain to you that my manager will return from town, and then you will get your money.

SMIRNOV: I did not come to see the manager; I came to see you. What the devil--pardon the language--do I care for your manager?

MRS. POPOV: Really, sir, I am not used to such language or such manners. I shan't listen to you any further.

[She goes out, left.]

SMIRNOV: What can one say to that? Moods! Seven months since her husband died! Do I have to pay the interest or not? I repeat the question, have I to pay the interest or not? The husband is dead and all that; the manager is--the devil with him!--traveling somewhere. Now, tell me, what am I to do? Shall I run away from my creditors in a balloon? Or knock my head against a stone wall? If I call on Grusdev he chooses to be "not at home," Iroschevitch has simply hidden himself, I have quarreled with Kurzin and came near throwing him out of the window, Masutov is ill and this woman has--moods! Not one of them will pay up! And all because I've spoiled them, because I'm an old whiner, dish-rag! I'm too tender-hearted with them. But wait! I allow nobody to play tricks with me, the devil with 'em all! I'll stay here and not budge until she pays! Brr! How angry I am, how terribly angry I am! Every tendon is trembling with anger, and I can hardly breathe! I'm even growing ill! *[He calls out.]* Servant!

[LUKA enters.]

LUKA: What is it you wish?

SMIRNOV: Bring me Kvas or water! *[LUKA goes out.]* Well, what can we do? She hasn't it on hand? What sort of logic is that? A fellow stands with the knife at his throat, he needs money, he is on the point of hanging himself, and she won't pay because she isn't in the mood to discuss money matters. Women's logic! That's why I never liked to talk to women, and why I dislike doing it now. I would rather sit on a powder barrel than talk with a woman. Brr!--I'm getting cold as ice; this affair has made me so angry. I need only to see such a romantic creature from a distance to get so angry that I have cramps in my calves! It's enough to make one yell for help!

[Enter LUKA.]

LUKA: *[Hands him water.]* Madam is ill and is not receiving.

SMIRNOV: March! *[LUKA goes out.]* Ill and isn't receiving! All right, it isn't necessary. I won't receive, either! I'll sit here and stay until you bring that money. If you're ill a week, I'll sit here a week. If you're ill a year, I'll sit here a year. As Heaven is my witness, I'll get the money. You don't disturb me with your mourning--or with your dimples. We know these dimples! *[He calls out the window.]* Simon, unharness! We aren't going to leave right away. I am going to stay here. Tell them in the stable to give the horses some oats. The left horse has twisted the bridle again. *[Imitating him.]* Stop! I'll show you how. Stop! *[Leaves window.]* It's awful. Unbearable heat, no money, didn't sleep last night and now--mourning-dresses with moods. My head aches; perhaps I ought to have a drink. Yes, I must have a drink. *[Calling.]* Servant!

LUKA: What do you wish?

SMIRNOV: Something to drink! *[LUKA goes out. SMIRNOV sits down and looks at his clothes.]* Ugh, a fine figure! No use denying that. Dust, dirty boots, unwashed, uncombed, straw on my vest--the lady probably took me for a highwayman. *[He yawns.]* It was a little impolite to come into a reception-room with such clothes. Oh, well, no harm done. I'm not here as a guest. I'm a creditor. And there is no special costume for creditors.

LUKA: *[Entering with glass.]* You take great liberty, sir.

SMIRNOV: *[Angrily.]* What?

LUKA: I--I--I just----

SMIRNOV: Whom are you talking to? Keep quiet.

LUKA: *[Angrily.]* Nice mess! This fellow won't leave!

[He goes out.]

SMIRNOV: Lord, how angry I am! Angry enough to throw mud at the whole world! I even feel ill! Servant!

[MRS. POPOV comes in with downcast eyes.]

MRS. POPOV: Sir, in my solitude I have become unaccustomed to the human voice and I cannot stand the sound of loud talking. I beg you, please to cease disturbing my rest.

SMIRNOV: Pay me my money and I'll leave.

MRS. POPOV: I told you once, plainly, in your native tongue, that I haven't the money at hand; wait until day after tomorrow.

SMIRNOV: And I also had the honor of informing you in your native tongue that I need the money, not day after tomorrow, but today. If you don't pay me today I shall have to hang myself tomorrow.

MRS. POPOV: But what can I do if I haven't the money?

SMIRNOV: So you are not going to pay immediately? You're not?

MRS. POPOV: I cannot.

SMIRNOV: Then I'll sit here until I get the money. *[He sits down.]* You will pay day after tomorrow? Excellent! Here I stay until day after tomorrow. *[Jumps up.]* I ask you, do I have to pay that interest tomorrow or not? Or do you think I'm joking?

MRS. POPOV: Sir, I beg of you, don't scream! This is not a stable.

SMIRNOV: I'm not talking about stables, I'm asking you whether I have to pay that interest to-morrow or not?

MRS. POPOV: You have no idea how to treat a lady.

SMIRNOV: Oh, yes, I have.

MRS. POPOV: No, you have not. You are an ill-bred, vulgar person! Respectable people don't speak so to ladies.

SMIRNOV: How remarkable! How do you want one to speak to you? In French, perhaps! Madame, *je vous prie!* Pardon me for having disturbed you. What beautiful weather we are having to-day! And how this mourning becomes you!

[He makes a low bow with mock ceremony.]

MRS. POPOV: Not at all funny! I think it vulgar!

SMIRNOV: *[Imitating her.]* Not at all funny--vulgar! I don't understand how to behave in the company of ladies. Madam, in the course of my life I have seen more women than you have sparrows. Three times have I fought duels for women, twelve I jilted and nine jilted me. There was a time when I played the fool, used honeyed language, bowed and scraped. I loved, suffered, sighed to the moon, melted in love's torments. I loved passionately, I loved to madness, loved in every key, chattered like a magpie on emancipation, sacrificed half my fortune in the tender passion, until now the devil knows I've had enough of it. Your obedient servant will let you lead him around by the nose no more. Enough! Black eyes, passionate eyes, coral lips, dimples in cheeks, moonlight whispers, soft, modest sights--for all that, madam, I wouldn't pay a kopeck! I am not speaking of present company, but of women in general; from the tiniest to the greatest, they are conceited, hypocritical, chattering, odious, deceitful from top to toe; vain, petty, cruel with a maddening logic and *[he strikes his forehead]* in this respect, please excuse my frankness, but one sparrow is worth ten of the aforementioned petticoat-philosophers. When one sees one of the romantic creatures before him he imagines he is looking at some holy being, so wonderful that its one breath could dissolve him in a sea of a thousand charms and delights; but if one looks into the soul--it's nothing but a common crocodile. *[He seizes the arm-chair and breaks it in two.]* But the worst of all is that this crocodile imagines it is a masterpiece of creation, and that it has a monopoly on all the tender passions. May the devil hang me upside down if there is anything to love about a woman! When she is in love, all she knows is how to complain and shed tears. If the man suffers and makes sacrifices she swings her train about and tries to lead him by the nose. You have the misfortune to be a woman, and naturally you know woman's nature; tell me on your honor, have you ever in your life seen a woman who was really true and faithful? Never! Only the old and the deformed are true and faithful. It's easier to find a cat with horns or a white woodcock, than a faithful woman.

MRS. POPOV: But allow me to ask, who is true and faithful in love? The man, perhaps?

SMIRNOV: Yes, indeed! The man!

MRS. POPOV: The man! *[She laughs sarcastically.]* The man true and faithful in love! Well, that is something *new! [Bitterly.]* How cán you make such a statement? Men true and faithful! So long as we have gone thus far, I may as well say that of all the men I have known, my husband was the best; I loved him passionately with all my soul, as only a young, sensible woman may love; I gave him my youth, my happiness, my fortune, my life. I worshipped him like a heathen. And what happened? This best of men betrayed me in every possible way. After his death I found his desk filled with love-letters. While he was alive he left me alone for months--it is horrible even to think about it--he made love to other women in my very presence, he wasted my money and made fun of my feelings--and in spite of everything I trusted him and was true to him. And more than that: he is dead and I am still true to him. I have buried myself within these four walls and I shall wear this mourning to my grave.

SMIRNOV: *[Laughing disrespectfully.]* Mourning! What on earth do you take me for? As if I didn't know why you wore this black domino and why you buried yourself within these four walls. Such a secret! So romantic! Some knight will pass the castle, gaze up at the windows, and think to himself: "Here dwells the mysterious Tamara who, for love of her husband, has buried herself within four walls." Oh, I understand the art!

MRS. POPOV: *[Springing up.]* What? What do you mean by saying such things to me?

SMIRNOV: You have buried yourself alive, but meanwhile you have not forgotten to powder your nose!

MRS. POPOV: How dare you speak so?

SMIRNOV: Don't scream at me, please; I'm not the manager. Allow me to call things by their right names. I am not a woman, and I am accustomed to speak out what I think. So please don't scream.

MRS. POPOV: I'm not screaming. It is you who are screaming. Please leave me, I beg you.

SMIRNOV: Pay me my money, and I'll leave.

MRS. POPOV: I won't give you the money.

SMIRNOV: You won't? You won't give me my money?

MRS. POPOV: I don't care what you do. You won't get a kopeck! Leave me!

SMIRNOV: As I haven't had the pleasure of being either your husband or your fiancé, please don't make a scene. *[He sits down.]* I can't stand it.

MRS. POPOV: *[Breathing hard.]* You are going to sit down?

SMIRNOV: I already have.

MRS. POPOV: Kindly leave the house!

SMIRNOV: Give me the money.

MRS. POPOV: I don't care to speak with impudent men. Leave! *[Pause.]* You aren't going?

SMIRNOV: No.

MRS. POPOV: No?

SMIRNOV: No.

MRS. POPOV: Very well.

[She rings the bell. Enter LUKA.]

MRS. POPOV: Luka, show the gentleman out.

LUKA: *[Going to SMIRNOV.]* Sir, why don't you leave when you are ordered? What do you want?

SMIRNOV: *[Jumping up.]* Whom do you think you are talking to? I'll grind you to powder.

LUKA: *[Puts his hand to his heart.]* Good Lord! *[He drops into a chair.]* Oh, I'm ill; I can't breathe!

MRS. POPOV: Where is Dascha? *[Calling.]* Dascha! Pelageja! Dascha!

[She rings.]

LUKA: They're all gone! I'm ill! Water!

MRS. POPOV: *[To SMIRNOV.]* Leave! Get out!

SMIRNOV: Kindly be a little more polite!

MRS. POPOV: *[Striking her fists and stamping her feet.]* You are vulgar! You're a boor! A monster!

SMIRNOV: What did you say?

MRS. POPOV: I said you were a boor, a monster!

SMIRNOV: *[Steps toward her quickly.]* Permit me to ask what right you have to insult me?

MRS. POPOV: What of it? Do you think I am afraid of you?

SMIRNOV: And you think that because you are a romantic creature you can insult me without being punished? I challenge you!

LUKA: Merciful Heaven! Water!

SMIRNOV: We'll have a duel!

MRS. POPOV: Do you think because you have big fists and a steer's neck I am afraid of you?

SMIRNOV: I allow no one to insult me, and I make no exception because you are a woman, one of the "weaker sex!"

MRS. POPOV: *[Trying to cry him down.]* Boor, boor, boor!

SMIRNOV: It is high time to do away with the old superstition that it is only the man who is forced to give satisfaction. If there is equity at all let there be equity in all things. There's a limit!

MRS. POPOV: You wish to fight a duel? Very well.

SMIRNOV: Immediately.

MRS. POPOV: Immediately. My husband had pistols. I'll bring them. *[She hurries away, then turns.]* Oh, what a pleasure it will be to put a bullet in your impudent head. The devil take you!

[She goes out.]

SMIRNOV: I'll shoot her down! I'm no fledgling, no sentimental young puppy. For me there is no weaker sex!

LUKA: Oh, sir. *[Falls to his knees.]* Have mercy on me, an old man, and go away. You have frightened me to death already, and now you want to fight a duel.

SMIRNOV: *[Paying no attention.]* A duel. That's equity, emancipation. That way the sexes are made equal. I'll shoot her down as a matter of principle. What can a person say to such a woman? *[Imitating her.]* "The devil take you. I'll put a bullet in your impudent head." What can one say to that? She was angry, her eyes blazed, she accepted the challenge. On my honor, it's the first time in my life that I ever saw such a woman.

LUKA: Oh, sir. Go away. Go away!

SMIRNOV: That *is* a woman. I can understand her. A real woman. No shilly-shallying, but fire, powder, and noise! It would be a pity to shoot a woman like that.

LUKA: *[Weeping.]* Oh, sir, go away.

[Enter MRS. POPOV.]

MRS. POPOV: Here are the pistols. But before we have our duel, please show me how to shoot. I have never had a pistol in my hand before!

LUKA: God be merciful and have pity upon us! I'll go and get the gardener and the coachman. Why has this horror come to us?

[He goes out.]

SMIRNOV: *[Looking at the pistols.]* You see, there are different kinds. There are special dueling pistols, with cap and ball. But these are revolvers, Smith & Wesson, with ejectors; fine pistols! A pair like that cost at least ninety roubles. This is the way to hold a revolver. *[Aside.]* Those eyes, those eyes! A real woman!

MRS. POPOV: Like this?

SMIRNOV: Yes, that way. Then you pull the hammer back--so--then you aim--put your head back a little. Just stretch your arm out, please. So--then press your finger on the thing like that, and that is all. The chief thing is this: don't get excited, don't hurry your aim, and take care that your hand doesn't tremble.

MRS. POPOV: It isn't well to shoot inside; let's go into the garden.

SMIRNOV: Yes. I'll tell you now, I am going to shoot into the air.

MRS. POPOV: That is too much! Why?

SMIRNOV: Because---because. That's my business.

MRS. POPOV: You are afraid. Yes. A-h-h-h. No, no, my dear sir, no flinching! Please follow me. I won't rest until I've made a hole in that head I hate so much. Are you afraid?

SMIRNOV: Yes, I'm afraid.

MRS. POPOV: You are lying. Why won't you fight?

SMIRNOV: Because--because--I--like you.

MRS. POPOV: *[With an angry laugh.]* You like me! He dares to say he likes me! *[She points to the door.]* Go.

SMIRNOV: *[Laying the revolver silently on the table, takes his hat and starts. At the door he stops a moment, gazing at her silently, then he approaches her, hesitating.]* Listen! Are you still angry? I was mad as the devil, but please understand me--how can I express myself? The thing is like this--such things are-- *[He raises his voice.]* Now, is it my fault that you owe me money? *[Grasps the back of the chair, which breaks.]* The devil know what breakable furniture you have! I like you! Do you understand? I--I'm almost in love!

MRS. POPOV: Leave! I hate you.

SMIRNOV: Lord! What a woman! I never in my life met one like her. I'm lost, ruined! I've been caught like a mouse in a trap.

MRS. POPOV: Go, or I'll shoot.

SMIRNOV: Shoot! You have no idea what happiness it would be to die in sight of those beautiful eyes, to die from the revolver in this little velvet hand! I'm mad! Consider it and decide immediately, for if I go now, we shall never see each other again. Decide--speak--I am a noble, a respectable man, have an income of ten thousand, can shoot a coin thrown into the air. I own some fine horses. Will you be my wife?

MRS. POPOV: *[Swings the revolver angrily.]* I'll shoot!

SMIRNOV: My mind is not clear--I can't understand. Servant--water! I have fallen in love like any young man. *[He takes her hand and she cries with pain.]* I love you! *[He kneels.]* I love you as I have never loved before. Twelve women I jilted, nine jilted me, but not one of them all have I loved as I love you. I am conquered, lost; I lie at your feet like a fool and beg for your hand. Shame and disgrace! For five years I haven't been in love; I thanked the Lord for it, and now I am caught, like a carriage tongue in another carriage. I beg for your hand! Yes or no? Will you?--Good!

[He gets up and goes quickly to the door.]

MRS. POPOV: Wait a minute!

SMIRNOV: *[Stopping.]* Well?

MRS. POPOV: Nothing. You may go. But--wait a moment. No, go on, go on. I hate you. Or--no; don't go. Oh, if you knew how angry I was, how angry! *[She throws the revolver on to the chair.]* My finger is swollen from this thing. *[She angrily tears her handkerchief.]* What are you standing there for? Get out!

SMIRNOV: Farewell!

MRS. POPOV: Yes, go. *[Cries out.]* Why are you going? Wait--no, go!! Oh, how angry I am! Don't come too near, don't come too near--er--come-- no nearer.

SMIRNOV: *[Approaching her.]* How angry I am with myself! Fall in love like a schoolboy, throw myself on my knees. I've got a chill! *[Strongly.]* I love you. This is fine--all I needed was to fall in love. Tomorrow I have to pay my interest, the hay harvest has begun, and then you appear! *[He takes her in his arms.]* I can never forgive myself.

MRS. POPOV: Go away! Take your hands off me! I hate you--you--this is--

[A long kiss. Enter LUKA with an axe, the gardener with a rake, the coachman with a pitchfork, and workmen with poles.]

LUKA: *[Staring at the pair.]* Merciful heavens!

[A long pause.]

MRS. POPOV: *[Dropping her eyes.]* Tell them in the stable that Tobby isn't to have any oats.

CURTAIN

TRIFLES

Susan Glaspell

CHARACTERS:

GEORGE HENDERSON, County Attorney
HENRY PETERS, Sheriff
LEWIS HALE, A neighboring farmer
MRS. PETERS
MRS. HALE

[The kitchen in the now abandoned farmhouse of JOHN WRIGHT, a gloomy kitchen, and left without having been put in order—unwashed pans under the sink, a loaf of bread outside the bread-box, a dish-towel on the table— other signs of incompleted work. At the rear the outer door opens and the SHERIFF comes in followed by the COUNTY ATTORNEY and HALE. The SHERIFF and HALE are men in middle life, the COUNTY ATTORNEY is a young man; all are much bundled up and go at once to the stove. They are followed by the two women—the SHERIFF's wife first; she is a slight wiry woman, a thin nervous face. MRS HALE is larger and would ordinarily be called more comfortable looking, but she is disturbed now and looks fearfully about as she enters. The women have come in slowly, and stand close together near the door.]

COUNTY ATTORNEY: *(rubbing his hands)* This feels good. Come up to the fire, ladies.

MRS. PETERS: *(after taking a step forward)* I'm not—cold.

SHERIFF: *(unbuttoning his overcoat and stepping away from the stove as if to mark the beginning of official business)* Now, Mr. Hale, before we move things about, you explain to Mr. Henderson just what you saw when you came here yesterday morning.

COUNTY ATTORNEY: By the way, has anything been moved? Are things just as you left them yesterday?

SHERIFF: *(looking about)* It's just the same. When it dropped below zero last night I thought I'd better send Frank out this morning to make a fire for us—no use getting pneumonia with a big case on, but I told him not to touch anything except the stove—and you know Frank.

COUNTY ATTORNEY: Somebody should have been left here yesterday.

SHERIFF: Oh—yesterday. When I had to send Frank to Morris Center for that man who went crazy—I want you to know I had my hands full yesterday. I knew you could get back from Omaha by today and as long as I went over everything here myself—

COUNTY ATTORNEY: Well, Mr. Hale, tell just what happened when you came here yesterday morning.

HALE: Harry and I had started to town with a load of potatoes. We came along the road from my place and as I got here I said 'I'm going to see if I can't get John Wright to go in with me on a party telephone.' I spoke to Wright about it once before and he put me off, saying folks talked too much anyway, and all he asked was peace and quiet—I guess you know about how much he talked himself; but I thought maybe if I went to the house and talked about it before his wife, though I said to Harry that I didn't know as what his wife wanted made much difference to John—

COUNTY ATTORNEY: Let's talk about that later, Mr. Hale. I do want to talk about that, but tell now just what happened when you got to the house.

HALE: I didn't hear or see anything; I knocked at the door, and still it was all quiet inside. I knew they must be up, it was past eight o'clock. So I knocked again, and I thought I heard somebody say, 'Come in.' I wasn't sure, I'm not sure yet, but I opened the door—this door *(indicating the door by which the two women are still standing)* and there in that rocker—*(pointing to it)* sat Mrs. Wright.

[They all look at the rocker.]

COUNTY ATTORNEY: What—was she doing?

HALE: She was rockin' back and forth. She had her apron in her hand and was kind of—pleating it.

COUNTY ATTORNEY: And how did she—look?

HALE: Well, she looked queer.

COUNTY ATTORNEY: How do you mean—queer?

HALE: Well, as if she didn't know what she was going to do next. And kind of done up.

COUNTY ATTORNEY: How did she seem to feel about your coming?

HALE: Why, I don't think she minded—one way or other. She didn't pay much attention. I said, 'How do, Mrs. Wright--it's cold, ain't it?' And she said, 'Is it?'—and went on kind of pleating at her apron. Well, I was surprised; she didn't ask me to come up to the stove, or to set down, but just sat there, not even looking at me, so I said, 'I want to see John.' And then she—laughed. I guess you would call it a laugh. I thought of Harry and the team outside, so I said a little sharp: 'Can't I see John?' 'No', she says, kind o' dull like. 'Ain't he home?' says I. 'Yes', says she, 'he's home'. 'Then why can't I see him?' I asked her, out of patience. ''Cause he's dead', says she. 'Dead?' says I. She just nodded her head, not getting a bit excited, but rockin' back and forth. 'Why—where is he?' says I, not knowing what to say. She just pointed upstairs—like that *(himself pointing to the room above)*. I got up, with the idea of going up there. I walked from there to here—then I says, 'Why, what did he die of?' 'He died of a rope round his neck', says she, and just went on pleatin' at her apron. Well, I went out and called Harry. I thought I might—need help. We went upstairs and there he was lyin'—

COUNTY ATTORNEY: I think I'd rather have you go into that upstairs, where you can point it all out. Just go on now with the rest of the story.

HALE: Well, my first thought was to get that rope off. It looked ... *(stops, his face twitches)* ... but Harry, he went up to him, and he said, 'No, he's dead all right, and we'd better not touch anything.' So we went back down stairs. She was still sitting that same way. 'Has anybody been notified?' I asked. 'No', says she unconcerned. 'Who did this, Mrs. Wright?' said Harry. He said it business-like—and she stopped pleatin' of her apron. 'I don't know', she says. 'You don't know?' says Harry. 'No', says she. 'Weren't you sleepin' in the bed with him?' says Harry. 'Yes', says she, 'but I was on the inside'. 'Somebody slipped a rope round his neck and strangled him and you didn't wake up?' says Harry. 'I didn't wake up', she said after him. We must 'a looked as if we didn't see how that could be, for after a minute she said, 'I sleep sound'. Harry was going to ask her more questions but I said maybe we ought to let her tell her story first to the coroner, or the sheriff, so Harry went fast as he could to Rivers' place, where there's a telephone.

COUNTY ATTORNEY: And what did Mrs. Wright do when she knew that you had gone for the coroner?

HALE: She moved from that chair to this one over here *(pointing to a small chair in the corner)* and just sat there with her hands held together and looking down. I got a feeling that I ought to make some conversation, so I said I had come in to see if John wanted to put in a telephone, and at that she started to laugh, and then she stopped and looked at me—scared, *(the COUNTY ATTORNEY, who has had his notebook out, makes a note)*. I dunno, maybe it wasn't scared. I wouldn't like to say it was. Soon Harry got back, and then Dr. Lloyd came, and you, Mr. Peters, and so I guess that's all I know that you don't.

COUNTY ATTORNEY: *(looking around)* I guess we'll go upstairs first—and then out to the barn and around there. *(to the SHERIFF)* You're convinced that there was nothing important here—nothing that would point to any motive.

SHERIFF: Nothing here but kitchen things.

[The COUNTY ATTORNEY, after again looking around the kitchen, opens the door of a cupboard closet. He gets up on a chair and looks on a shelf. Pulls his hand away, sticky.]

COUNTY ATTORNEY: Here's a nice mess.

[The women draw nearer.]

MRS. PETERS: *(to the other woman)* Oh, her fruit; it did freeze. *(to the LAWYER)* She worried about that when it turned so cold. She said the fire'd go out and her jars would break.

SHERIFF: Well, can you beat the women! Held for murder and worryin' about her preserves.

COUNTY ATTORNEY: I guess before we're through she may have something more serious than preserves to worry about.

HALE: Well, women are used to worrying over trifles.

[The two women move a little closer together.]

COUNTY ATTORNEY: *(with the gallantry of a young politician)* And yet, for all their worries, what would we do without the ladies? *(The women do not unbend. He goes to the sink, takes a dipperful of water from the pail and pouring it into a basin, washes his hands. Starts to wipe them on the roller-towel, turns it for a cleaner place.)* Dirty towels! *(Kicks his foot against the pans under the sink.)* Not much of a housekeeper, would you say, ladies?

MRS. HALE: *(stiffly)* There's a great deal of work to be done on a farm.

COUNTY ATTORNEY: To be sure. And yet *(with a little bow to her)* I know there are some Dickson county farmhouses which do not have such roller towels. *(He gives it a pull to expose its length again.)*

MRS. HALE: Those towels get dirty awful quick. Men's hands aren't always as clean as they might be.

COUNTY ATTORNEY: Ah, loyal to your sex, I see. But you and Mrs. Wright were neighbors. I suppose you were friends, too.

MRS. HALE: *(shaking her head)* I've not seen much of her of late years. I've not been in this house—it's more than a year.

COUNTY ATTORNEY: And why was that? You didn't like her?

MRS. HALE: I liked her well enough. Farmers' wives have their hands full, Mr. Henderson. And then—

COUNTY ATTORNEY: Yes—?

MRS. HALE: *(looking about)* It never seemed a very cheerful place.

COUNTY ATTORNEY: No—it's not cheerful. I shouldn't say she had the homemaking instinct.

MRS. HALE: Well, I don't know as Wright had, either.

COUNTY ATTORNEY: You mean that they didn't get on very well?

MRS. HALE: No, I don't mean anything. But I don't think a place'd be any cheerfuller for John Wright's being in it.

COUNTY ATTORNEY: I'd like to talk more of that a little later. I want to get the lay of things upstairs now. *(He goes to the left, where three steps lead to a stair door.)*

SHERIFF: I suppose anything Mrs. Peters does'll be all right. She was to take in some clothes for her, you know, and a few little things. We left in such a hurry yesterday.

COUNTY ATTORNEY: Yes, but I would like to see what you take, Mrs. Peters, and keep an eye out for anything that might be of use to us.

MRS. PETERS: Yes, Mr. Henderson.

[The women listen to the men's steps on the stairs, then look about the kitchen.]

MRS. HALE: I'd hate to have men coming into my kitchen, snooping around and criticizing.

[She arranges the pans under sink which the LAWYER had shoved out of place.]

MRS. PETERS: Of course it's no more than their duty.

MRS. HALE: Duty's all right, but I guess that deputy sheriff that came out to make the fire might have got a little of this on. *(Gives the roller towel a pull.)* Wish I'd thought of that sooner. Seems mean to talk about her for not having things slicked up when she had to come away in such a hurry.

MRS. PETERS: *(who has gone to a small table in the left rear corner of the room, and lifted one end of a towel that covers a pan)* She had bread set. *(Stands still.)*

MRS. HALE: *(eyes fixed on a loaf of bread beside the bread-box, which is on a low shelf at the other side of the room. Moves slowly toward it.)* She was going to put this in there. *(Picks up loaf, then abruptly drops it. In a manner of returning to familiar things.)* It's a shame about her fruit. I wonder if it's all gone. *(Gets up on the chair and looks.)* I think there's some here that's all right, Mrs. Peters. Yes—here; *(holding it toward the window)* this is cherries, too. *(looking again)* I declare I believe that's the only one. *(Gets down, bottle in her hand. Goes to the sink and wipes it off on the outside)* She'll feel awful bad after all her hard work in the hot weather. I remember the afternoon I put up my cherries last summer.

[She puts the bottle on the big kitchen table, center of the room. With a sigh, is about to sit down in the rocking-chair. Before she is seated realizes what chair it is; with a slow look at it, steps back. The chair which she has touched rocks back and forth.]

MRS. PETERS: Well, I must get those things from the front room closet. *(She goes to the door at the right, but after looking into the other room, steps back.)* You coming with me, Mrs. Hale? You could help me carry them.

[They go in the other room; reappear, MRS. PETERS carrying a dress and skirt, MRS. HALE following with a pair of shoes.]

MRS. PETERS: My, it's cold in there.

[She puts the clothes on the big table, and hurries to the stove.]

MRS. HALE: *(examining the skirt)* Wright was close. I think maybe that's why she kept so much to herself. She didn't even belong to the Ladies Aid. I suppose she felt she couldn't do her part, and then you don't enjoy things when you feel shabby. She used to wear pretty clothes and be lively, when she was Minnie Foster, one of the town girls singing in the choir. But that— oh, that was thirty years ago. This all you was to take in?

MRS. PETERS: She said she wanted an apron. Funny thing to want, for there isn't much to get you dirty in jail, goodness knows. But I suppose just to make her feel more natural. She said they was in the top drawer in this cupboard. Yes, here. And then her little shawl that always hung behind the door. *(Opens stair door and looks.)* Yes, here it is.

[Quickly shuts door leading upstairs.]

MRS. HALE: *(abruptly moving toward her)* Mrs. Peters?

MRS. PETERS: Yes, Mrs. Hale?

MRS. HALE: Do you think she did it?

MRS. PETERS: *(in a frightened voice)* Oh, I don't know.

MRS. HALE: Well, I don't think she did. Asking for an apron and her little shawl. Worrying about her fruit.

MRS. PETERS: *(starts to speak, glances up, where footsteps are heard in the room above. In a low voice)* Mr. Peters says it looks bad for her. Mr. Henderson is awful sarcastic in speech and he'll make fun of her sayin' she didn't wake up.

MRS. HALE: Well, I guess John Wright didn't wake when they was slipping that rope under his neck.

MRS. PETERS: No, it's strange. It must have been done awful crafty and still. They say it was such a—funny way to kill a man, rigging it all up like that.

MRS. HALE: That's just what Mr. Hale said. There was a gun in the house. He says that's what he can't understand.

MRS. PETERS: Mr. Henderson said coming out that what was needed for the case was a motive; something to show anger, or—sudden feeling.

MRS. HALE: *(who is standing by the table)* Well, I don't see any signs of anger around here. *(She puts her hand on the dish towel which lies on the table, stands looking down at table, one half of which is clean, the other half messy.)* It's wiped to here. *(Makes a move as if to finish work, then turns and looks at loaf of bread outside the breadbox. Drops towel. In that voice of coming back to familiar things)* Wonder how they are finding things upstairs. I hope she had it a little more red-up up there. You know, it seems kind of sneaking. Locking her up in town and then coming out here and trying to get her own house to turn against her!

MRS. PETERS: But Mrs. Hale, the law is the law.

MRS. HALE: I s'pose 'tis. *(unbuttoning her coat)* Better loosen up your things, Mrs. Peters. You won't feel them when you go out.

[MRS. PETERS takes off her fur tippet, goes to hang it on hook at back of room, stands looking at the under part of the small corner table.]

MRS. PETERS: She was piecing a quilt.

[She brings the large sewing basket and they look at the bright pieces.]

MRS. HALE: It's a log cabin pattern. Pretty, isn't it? I wonder if she was goin' to quilt it or just knot it?

[Footsteps have been heard coming down the stairs. The SHERIFF enters followed by HALE and the COUNTY ATTORNEY.]

SHERIFF: They wonder if she was going to quilt it or just knot it!

[The men laugh, the women look abashed.]

COUNTY ATTORNEY: *(rubbing his hands over the stove)* Frank's fire didn't do much up there, did it? Well, let's go out to the barn and get that cleared up. *(The men go outside.)*

MRS. HALE: *(resentfully)* I don't know as there's anything so strange, our takin' up our time with little things while we're waiting for them to get the evidence. *(She sits down at the big table smoothing out a block with decision.)* I don't see as it's anything to laugh about.

MRS. PETERS: *(apologetically)* Of course they've got awful important things on their minds.

[Pulls up a chair and joins MRS. HALE at the table.]

MRS. HALE: *(examining another block)* Mrs. Peters, look at this one. Here, this is the one she was working on, and look at the sewing! All the rest of it has been so nice and even. And look at this! It's all over the place! Why, it looks as if she didn't know what she was about!

[After she has said this they look at each other, then start to glance back at the door. After an instant MRS. HALE has pulled at a knot and ripped the sewing.]

MRS. PETERS: Oh, what are you doing, Mrs. Hale?

MRS. HALE: *(mildly)* Just pulling out a stitch or two that's not sewed very good. *(threading a needle)* Bad sewing always made me fidgety.

MRS. PETERS: *(nervously)* I don't think we ought to touch things.

MRS. HALE: I'll just finish up this end. *(suddenly stopping and leaning forward)* Mrs. Peters?

MRS. PETERS: Yes, Mrs. Hale?

MRS. HALE: What do you suppose she was so nervous about?

MRS. PETERS: Oh—I don't know. I don't know as she was nervous. I sometimes sew awful queer when I'm just tired. *(MRS. HALE starts to say something, looks at MRS. PETERS, then goes on sewing.)* Well I must get these things wrapped up. They may be through sooner than we think.

(putting apron and other things together) I wonder where I can find a piece of paper, and string.

MRS. HALE: In that cupboard, maybe.

MRS. PETERS: *(looking in cupboard)* Why, here's a bird-cage. *(Holds it up.)* Did she have a bird, Mrs. Hale?

MRS. HALE: Why, I don't know whether she did or not—I've not been here for so long. There was a man around last year selling canaries cheap, but I don't know as she took one; maybe she did. She used to sing real pretty herself.

MRS. PETERS: *(glancing around)* Seems funny to think of a bird here. But she must have had one, or why would she have a cage? I wonder what happened to it.

MRS. HALE: I s'pose maybe the cat got it.

MRS. PETERS: No, she didn't have a cat. She's got that feeling some people have about cats—being afraid of them. My cat got in her room and she was real upset and asked me to take it out.

MRS. HALE: My sister Bessie was like that. Queer, ain't it?

MRS. PETERS: *(examining the cage)* Why, look at this door. It's broke. One hinge is pulled apart.

MRS. HALE: *(looking too)* Looks as if someone must have been rough with it.

MRS. PETERS: Why, yes.

[She brings the cage forward and puts it on the table.]

MRS. HALE: I wish if they're going to find any evidence they'd be about it. I don't like this place.

MRS. PETERS: But I'm awful glad you came with me, Mrs. Hale. It would be lonesome for me sitting here alone.

MRS. HALE: It would, wouldn't it? *(dropping her sewing)* But I tell you what I do wish, Mrs. Peters. I wish I had come over sometimes when she was here. I—*(looking around the room)*—wish I had.

MRS. PETERS: But of course you were awful busy, Mrs. Hale—your house and your children.

MRS. HALE: I could've come. I stayed away because it weren't cheerful—and that's why I ought to have come. I—I've never liked this place. Maybe because it's down in a hollow and you don't see the road. I dunno what it is, but it's a lonesome place and always was. I wish I had come over to see Minnie Foster sometimes. I can see now—*(Shakes her head.)*

MRS. PETERS: Well, you mustn't reproach yourself, Mrs. Hale. Somehow we just don't see how it is with other folks until—something comes up.

MRS. HALE: Not having children makes less work—but it makes a quiet house, and Wright out to work all day, and no company when he did come in. Did you know John Wright, Mrs. Peters?

MRS. PETERS: Not to know him; I've seen him in town. They say he was a good man.

MRS. HALE: Yes—good; he didn't drink, and kept his word as well as most, I guess, and paid his debts. But he was a hard man, Mrs. Peters. Just to pass the time of day with him—*(Shivers.)* Like a raw wind that gets to the bone. *(Pauses, her eye falling on the cage.)* I should think she would 'a wanted a bird. But what do you suppose went with it?

MRS. PETERS: I don't know, unless it got sick and died.

[She reaches over and swings the broken door, swings it again, both women watch it.]

MRS. HALE: You weren't raised round here, were you? *(MRS. PETERS shakes her head)* You didn't know—her?

MRS. PETERS: Not till they brought her yesterday.

MRS. HALE: She—come to think of it, she was kind of like a bird herself—real sweet and pretty, but kind of timid and—fluttery. How—she—did—change. *(Silence; then as if struck by a happy thought and relieved to get* back to everyday things.) Tell you what, Mrs. Peters, why don't you take the quilt in with you? It might take up her mind.

MRS. PETERS: Why, I think that's a real nice idea, Mrs. Hale. There couldn't possibly be any objection to it, could there? Now, just what would I take? I wonder if her patches are in here—and her things.

[They look in the sewing basket.]

MRS. HALE: Here's some red. I expect this has got sewing things in it. (Brings out a fancy box.) What a pretty box. Looks like something somebody would give you. Maybe her scissors are in here. (Opens box. Suddenly puts her hand to her nose.) Why—(MRS. PETERS bends nearer, then turns her face away.) There's something wrapped up in this piece of silk.

MRS. PETERS: Why, this isn't her scissors.

MRS. HALE: (lifting the silk) Oh, Mrs. Peters—it's—

[MRS. PETERS bends closer.]

MRS. PETERS: It's the bird.

MRS. HALE: (jumping up) But, Mrs. Peters—look at it! It's neck! Look at its neck! It's all—other side to.

MRS. PETERS: Somebody—wrung—its—neck.

[Their eyes meet. A look of growing comprehension, of horror. Steps are heard outside. MRS. HALE slips box under quilt pieces, and sinks into her chair. Enter SHERIFF and COUNTY ATTORNEY. MRS. PETERS rises.]

COUNTY ATTORNEY: (as one turning from serious things to little pleasantries) Well ladies, have you decided whether she was going to quilt it or knot it?

MRS. PETERS: We think she was going to—knot it.

COUNTY ATTORNEY: Well, that's interesting, I'm sure. (Seeing the birdcage.) Has the bird flown?

MRS. HALE: *(putting more quilt pieces over the box)* We think the—cat got it.

COUNTY ATTORNEY: *(preoccupied)* Is there a cat?

[MRS. HALE glances in a quick covert way at MRS. PETERS.]

MRS PETERS: Well, not now. They're superstitious, you know. They leave.

COUNTY ATTORNEY: *(to SHERIFF PETERS, continuing an interrupted conversation)* No sign at all of anyone having come from the outside. Their own rope. Now let's go up again and go over it piece by piece. *(They start upstairs.)* It would have to have been someone who knew just the—

[MRS. PETERS sits down. The two women sit there not looking at one another, but as if peering into something and at the same time holding back. When they talk now it is in the manner of feeling their way over strange ground, as if afraid of what they are saying, but as if they cannot help saying it.]

MRS. HALE: She liked the bird. She was going to bury it in that pretty box.

MRS. PETERS: *(in a whisper)* When I was a girl—my kitten—there was a boy took a hatchet, and before my eyes—and before I could get there— *(Covers her face an instant.)* If they hadn't held me back I would have— *(catches herself, looks upstairs where steps are heard, falters weakly)*—hurt him.

MRS. HALE: *(with a slow look around her)* I wonder how it would seem never to have had any children around. *(Pause.)* No, Wright wouldn't like the bird—a thing that sang. She used to sing. He killed that, too.

MRS. PETERS: *(moving uneasily)* We don't know who killed the bird.

MRS. HALE: I knew John Wright.

MRS. PETERS: It was an awful thing was done in this house that night, Mrs. Hale. Killing a man while he slept, slipping a rope around his neck that choked the life out of him.

MRS. HALE: His neck. Choked the life out of him.

[Her hand goes out and rests on the bird-cage.]

MRS. PETERS: *(with rising voice)* We don't know who killed him. We don't know.

MRS. HALE: *(her own feeling not interrupted)* If there'd been years and years of nothing, then a bird to sing to you, it would be awful—still, after the bird was still.

MRS. PETERS: *(something within her speaking)* I know what stillness is. When we homesteaded in Dakota, and my first baby died—after he was two years old, and me with no other then—

MRS. HALE: *(moving)* How soon do you suppose they'll be through, looking for the evidence?

MRS. PETERS: I know what stillness is. *(pulling herself back)* The law has got to punish crime, Mrs. Hale.

MRS. HALE: *(not as if answering that)* I wish you'd seen Minnie Foster when she wore a white dress with blue ribbons and stood up there in the choir and sang. *(A look around the room.)* Oh, I wish I'd come over here once in a while! That was a crime! That was a crime! Who's going to punish that?

MRS. PETERS: *(looking upstairs)* We mustn't—take on.

MRS. HALE: I might have known she needed help! I know how things can be—for women. I tell you, it's queer, Mrs. Peters. We live close together and we live far apart. We all go through the same things—it's all just a different kind of the same thing. *(Brushes her eyes, noticing the bottle of fruit, reaches out for it.)* If I was you, I wouldn't tell her her fruit was gone. Tell her it ain't. Tell her it's all right. Take this in to prove it to her. She—she may never know whether it was broke or not.

MRS. PETERS: *(takes the bottle, looks about for something to wrap it in; takes petticoat from the clothes brought from the other room, very nervously begins winding this around the bottle. In a false voice)* My, it's a good thing the men couldn't hear us. Wouldn't they just laugh! Getting all stirred up over a little thing like a—dead canary. As if that could have anything to do with—with—wouldn't they laugh!

[The men are heard coming down stairs.]

MRS. HALE: *(under her breath)* Maybe they would—maybe they wouldn't.

COUNTY ATTORNEY: No, Peters, it's all perfectly clear except a reason for doing it. But you know juries when it comes to women. If there was some definite thing. Something to show—something to make a story about—a thing that would connect up with this strange way of doing it—

[The women's eyes meet for an instant. Enter HALE from outer door.]

HALE: Well, I've got the team around. Pretty cold out there.

COUNTY ATTORNEY: I'm going to stay here a while by myself. *(to the SHERIFF)* You can send Frank out for me, can't you? I want to go over everything. I'm not satisfied that we can't do better.

SHERIFF: Do you want to see what Mrs. Peters is going to take in?

[The LAWYER goes to the table, picks up the apron, laughs.]

COUNTY ATTORNEY: Oh, I guess they're not very dangerous things the ladies have picked out. *(Moves a few things about, disturbing the quilt pieces which cover the box. Steps back.)* No, Mrs. Peters doesn't need supervising. For that matter, a sheriff's wife is married to the law. Ever think of it that way, Mrs. Peters?

MRS. PETERS: Not—just that way.

SHERIFF: *(chuckling)* Married to the law. *(Moves toward the other room.)* I just want you to come in here a minute, George. We ought to take a look at these windows.

COUNTY ATTORNEY: *(scoffingly)* Oh, windows!

SHERIFF: We'll be right out, Mr. Hale.

[HALE goes outside. The SHERIFF follows the COUNTY ATTORNEY into the other room. Then MRS. HALE rises, hands tight together, looking intensely at MRS. PETERS, whose eyes make a slow turn, finally meeting MRS. HALE's. A moment MRS. HALE holds her, then her own eyes point the way to where the box is concealed. Suddenly MRS. PETERS throws back

quilt pieces and tries to put the box in the bag she is wearing. It is too big. She opens box, starts to take bird out, cannot touch it, goes to pieces, stands there helpless. Sound of a knob turning in the other room. MRS. HALE snatches the box and puts it in the pocket of her big coat. Enter COUNTY ATTORNEY and SHERIFF.]

COUNTY ATTORNEY: *(facetiously)* Well, Henry, at least we found out that she was not going to quilt it. She was going to—what is it you call it, ladies?

MRS. HALE: *(her hand against her pocket)* We call it—knot it, Mr. Henderson.

CURTAIN

THE STRONGER

August Strindberg

Translated by Charles Wangel

CHARACTERS:

MME. X: an actress, married
MLLE. Y: an actress, single

SETTING:

The corner of a ladies' cafe, two little iron tables, a red velvet sofa, several chairs.

[MME. X enters, dressed in winter clothes, wearing hat and cloak and carrying a dainty Japanese basket on her arm. MLLE. Y sits beside a half-empty beer bottle, reading an illustrated newspaper which she later changes for another.]

MME. X: Good evening, Amelia, you're sitting here alone on Christmas Eve like a poor old maid. *[MLLE. Y glances up from the newspaper, nods, and resumes her reading.]* Do you know it worries me to see you this way, alone in a café, and on Christmas Eve, too. It makes me feel as I did that time when I saw a bridal party in a Paris restaurant, the bride sitting reading a comic paper, while the groom played billiards with the witnesses. Ah! thought I, with such a beginning, what a sequel and what an ending! He played billiards on his wedding evening--and she read a comic paper!--But that is neither here nor there. *[The WAITER enters, places a cup of Chocolate before MME. X and goes out.]* I tell you what, Amelia! I believe you would have done better to have kept him! Do you remember I was the first to say 'forgive him!' Recollect? Then you would have been married now and have had a home. Remember that Christmas in the country? How happy you were with your fiancé's parents, how you enjoyed the happiness of their home, yet longed for the theater. Yes, Amelia, dear, home is the best of all--next to the theater--and the children, you understand--but that you don't understand! *[MLLE. Y looks scornful. MME. X sips a spoonful out of the cup, then opens her basket and takes out the Christmas presents.]* Here you can see what I have bought for my little pigs. *[Takes up a doll]* Look at this! This is for Liza. See?--And here is Maja's pop gun. *[Loads and shoots at MLLE. Y who makes a startled gesture.]* Were you frightened? Do you think I should like to shoot you? What? My soul! I don't believe you thought that! If you wanted to shoot me, that wouldn't surprise me, because I came in your way--and that, I know, you can never forget. But I was quite innocent. You still believe I intrigued you out of the theater, but I didn't do that! I didn't do that even if you do think so. But it's all one whether I say so or not, for you still believe it was I! *[Takes up a pair of embroidered slippers.]* And these are for my old man. With tulips on them which I embroidered myself. I can't bear tulips, you know, but he must have tulips on everything. *[MLLE. Y looks up ironically and curiously. MME. X puts a hand in each slipper.]* See what little feet Bob has! What? And you ought to see how elegantly he walks! You've never seen him in slippers? *[MLLE. Y laughs aloud.]* Look here, this is he. *[She makes the slippers walk on the table. MLLE. Y laughs loudly.]* And when he is peeved, see, he stamps like this with his foot. 'What! Damn that cook, she never can learn to make coffee. Ah! Now those idiots haven't trimmed the lamp wick straight!' And then he wears out the soles and his feet freeze. 'Ugh, how cold it is and the stupid fools never can keep the fire in the heater.' *[She rubs together the slippers' soles and uppers.*

MLLE. Y laughs clearly.] And then he comes home and has to hunt for his slippers which Marie has stuck under the chiffonier. Oh, but it is a sin to sit here and make fun of one's husband. He's a pretty good little husband -- You ought to have such a husband, Amelia. What are you laughing at? What? What? -- And then I know he's true to me. Yes I know that. Because he told me himself. What are you tittering about? When I came back from my tour of Norway, that shameless Frederika came and wanted to elope with him. Can you imagine anything so infamous? *[Pause.]* But I'd have scratched her eyes out if she had come to see him when I was at home! *[Pause.]* It was good that Bob spoke of it himself and that it didn't reach me through gossip. *[Pause.]* But Frederika wasn't the only one, would you believe it! I don't know why, but women are crazy about my husband. They must think he has something to say about theater engagements because he's connected with the government. Perhaps you were there yourself and tried to influence him! I don't trust you any too much. But, I know he's not concerned about you, and you seem to have a grudge against him. *[Pause. They look quizzically at each other.]* Come to see us this evening, Amelia, and show that you're not angry with us -- not angry with me at any rate! I don't know why, but it's so uncomfortable to have you an enemy. Possibly it's because I came in your way *[rallentando]* or -- I really don't know -- just why. *[Pause. MLLE. Y stares at MME. X curiously.]* Our acquaintance has been so peculiar. *[Thoughtfully.]* When I saw you the first time I was so afraid of you, so afraid, that I couldn't look you in the face; still as I came and went I always found myself near you -- I couldn't risk being your enemy, so I became your friend. But there was always a discordant note when you came to our house, because I saw that my husband couldn't bear you -- and that was as annoying to me as an ill-fitting gown -- and I did all I could to make him friendly toward you, but before he consented you announced your engagement. Then came a violent friendship, so that in a twinkling it appeared as if you dared only show him your real feelings when you were betrothed -- and then -- how was it later? -- I didn't get jealous -- how wonderful! And I remember that when you were Patin's godmother, I made Bob kiss you -- he did it, but you were so confused -- that is, I didn't notice it then -- thought about it later -- never thought about it before -- now! *[Gets up hastily.]* Why are you silent? You haven't said a word this whole time, but you have let me go on talking! You have sat there and your eyes loosened out of me all these thoughts which lay like raw silk in their cocoon -- thoughts -- suspicious thoughts, perhaps -- let me see -- why did you break your engagement? Why do you come so seldom to our house these days? Why won't you visit us tonight? *[MLLE. Y appears as if about to speak.]* Keep still! You don't have to say anything. I comprehend it all myself! It was because, and because and because. Yes! Yes! Now everything is clear. So that's it! Pfui, I won't sit at the same table with you.

[Takes her things to the next table.] That's the reason why I had to embroider tulips, which I hate, on his slippers; because you are fond of tulips; that's why *[throws the slippers on the floor]* we go to the mountains during the summer, because you don't like the sea air; that's why my boy is named Eskil, because it's your father's name; that's why I wear your colors, read your authors, eat your pet dishes, drink your beverages--this chocolate, for example--that's why. Oh, my God, it's fearful, when I think about it; it's fearful! Everything, everything, came from you to me, even your passion! Your soul crept into mine, like a worm into an apple, ate and ate, grubbed and grubbed, until nothing was left but the rind within. I wanted to fly from you, but I couldn't; you lay like a snake and enchanted me with your black eyes--I felt as if the branch gave way and let me fall. I lay with feet bound together in the water and swam mightily with my hands, but the harder I struggled the deeper I worked myself under, until I sank to the bottom, where you lay like a giant crab ready to catch hold of me with your claws-- and I just lay there! Pfui! How I hate you! Hate you! Hate you! But you, you only sit there and keep silent, peacefully, indifferently, indifferent as to whether the moon waxes or wanes, whether it is Christmas or New Year, whether others are happy or unhappy, without the ability to hate or to love, as composed as a stork by a mouse hole. You can't make conquests yourself, you can't keep a man's love, but you can steal away that love from others! Here you sit in your corner--do you know they have named a mouse-trap after you?--and read your newspapers in order to see if anything has happened to any one, or who's had a run of bad luck, or who has left the theater; here you sit and review your work, calculating your mischief as a pilot does his course; collecting your tribute.... *[Pause.]* Poor Amelia, do you know that I'm really sorry for you, because you are so unhappy. Unhappy like a wounded animal, and spiteful because you are wounded! I can't be angry with you, no matter how much I want to be--because you come out at the small end of the horn. Yes; that affair with Bob--I don't care about that. What is that to me, after all? And if I learned to drink chocolate from you or from somebody else, what difference does it make. *[Drinks a spoonful out of the cup; knowingly.]* Besides, chocolate is very healthful. And if you taught me how to dress--*tant mieux*--that only makes me more attractive to my husband. And you lost what I won. Yes, to sum up: I believe you have lost him. But it was certainly your intent that I should go my own road--do as you did and regret as you now regret--but I don't do that! We won't be mean, will we? And why should I take only what nobody else will have? *[Pause.]* Possibly, all in all, at this moment I am really the stronger. You get nothing from me, but you gave me much. And now I appear like a thief to you. You wake up and find I possess what you have lost! How was it that everything in your hands was worthless and sterile? You can hold no man's love with your tulips and your passion, as I can. You

can't learn housekeeping from your authors, as I have done; you have no little Eskil to cherish, even if your father was named Eskil! And why do you keep silent, silent, silent? I believe that is strength, but, perhaps, it's because you have nothing to say! Because you don't think anything. *[Rises and gathers up her slippers.]* Now I'm going home--and take the tulips with me-- your tulips! You can't learn from another, you can't bend--and therefore you will be broken like a dry stalk--but I won't be! Thank you, Amelia, for all your good lessons. Thanks because you taught me to love my husband! Now I'll go home and love him!

[She goes.]

CURTAIN

ENEMIES

Neith Boyce and Hutchins Hapgood

CHARACTERS:

HE
SHE

SCENE: A Living-room

TIME: After Dinner

[SHE is lying in a long chair, smoking a cigarette and reading a book. HE is sitting at a table with a lamp at his left--manuscript pages scattered before him, pen in hand. He glances at her, turns the lamp up, turns it down, rustles his MS., snorts impatiently. She continues reading.]

HE: This is the limit!

SHE: *[calmly]* What is?

HE: Oh, nothing. *[She turns the page, continues reading with interest.]* This is an infernal lamp!

SHE: What's the matter with the lamp?

HE: I've asked you a thousand times to have some order in the house, some regularity, some system! The lamps never have oil, the wicks are never cut, the chimneys are always smoked! And yet you wonder that I don't work more! How can a man work without light?

SHE: *[glancing critically at the lamp]* This lamp seems to me to be all right. It obviously has oil in it or it would not burn, and the chimney is not smoked. As to the wick, I trimmed it myself today.

HE: Ah, that accounts for it.

SHE: Well, do it yourself next time, my dear!

HE: *[irritated]* But our time is too valuable for these ever-recurring jobs! Why don't you train Theresa, as I've asked you so often?

SHE: It would take all my time for a thousand years to train Theresa.

HE: Oh, I know! All you want to do is to lie in bed for breakfast, smoke cigarettes, write your high literary stuff, make love to other men, talk cleverly when you go out to dinner and never say a word to me at home! No wonder you have no time to train Theresa!

SHE: Is there anything of interest in the paper?

HE: You certainly have a nasty way of making an innocent remark!

SHE: *[absorbed in her book]* I'm sorry.

HE: No, you're not. The last remark proves it.

SHE: *[absently]* Proves what?

HE: Proves that you are an unsocial, brutal woman!

SHE: You are in a temper again.

HE: Who wouldn't be, to live with a cold-blooded person that you have to hit with a gridiron to get a rise out of?

SHE: I wish you would read your paper quietly and let me alone.

HE: Why have you lived with me for fifteen years if you want to be let alone?

SHE: *[with a sigh]* I have always hoped you would settle down.

HE: By settling down you mean cease bothering about household matters, about the children, cease wanting to be with you, cease expecting you to have any interest in me.

SHE: No, I only meant it would be nice to have a peaceful evening sometimes. But *[laying book down]* I see you want to quarrel--so what shall we quarrel about? Choose your own subject, my dear.

HE: When you're with Hank you don't want a peaceful evening!

SHE: Now how can you possibly know that?

HE: Oh, I've seen you with him and others and I know the difference. When you're with them you're alert and interested. You keep your unsociability for me. *[Pause.]* Of course, I know why.

SHE: One reason is that "they" don't talk about lamp-wicks and so forth. They talk about higher things.

HE: Some people would call them lower things!

SHE: Well--more interesting things, anyway.

HE: Yes, I know you think those things more interesting than household and children and husband.

SHE: Oh, only occasionally, you know--just for a change. You like a change yourself sometimes.

HE: Yes, sometimes. But I am excited, and interested and keen whenever I am with you. It is not only cigarettes and flirtation that excite me.

SHE: Well, you are an excitable person. You get excited about nothing at all.

HE: Are home and wife and children nothing at all?

SHE: There are other things. But you, Deacon, are like the skylark--
"Type of the wise who soar but do not roam--
True to the kindred points of heaven and home."

HE: You are cheaply cynical! You ought not to insult Wordsworth. He meant what he said.

SHE: He was a good man.... But to get back to our original quarrel. You're quite mistaken. I'm more social with you than with anyone else. Hank, for instance, hates to talk--even more than I do. He and I spend hours together looking at the sea--each of us absorbed in our own thoughts--without saying a word. What could be more peaceful than that?

HE: *[indignantly]* I don't believe it's peaceful--but it must be wonderful!

SHE: It is--marvelous. I wish you were more like that. What beautiful evenings we could have together!

HE: *[bitterly]* Most of our evenings are silent enough--unless we are quarreling!

SHE: Yes, if you're not talking, it's because you're sulking. You are never sweetly silent--never really quiet.

HE: That's true--with you--I am rarely quiet with you--because you rarely express anything to me. I would be more quiet if you were less so--less expressive if you were more so.

SHE: *[pensively]* The same old quarrel. Just the same for fifteen years! And all because you are you and I am I! And I suppose it will go on forever--I shall go on being silent, and you--

HE: I suppose I shall go on talking--but it really doesn't matter--the silence or the talk--if we had something to be silent about or to talk about--something in common--that's the point!

SHE: Do you really think we have nothing in common? We both like Dostoyevsky and prefer Burgundy to champagne.

HE: Our tastes and our vices are remarkably congenial, but our souls do not touch.

SHE: Our souls? Why should they? Every soul is lonely.

HE: Yes, but doesn't want to be. The soul desires to find something into which to fuse and so lose its loneliness. This hope to lose the soul's loneliness by union--is love. It is the essence of love as it is of religion.

SHE: Deacon, you are growing more holy every day. You will drive me to drink.

HE: *[moodily]* That will only complete the list.

SHE: Well, then I suppose we may be more congenial--for in spite of what you say, our vices haven't exactly matched. You're ahead of me on the drink.

HE: Yes, and you on some other things. But perhaps I can catch up, too--

SHE: Perhaps--if you really give all your time to it, as you did last winter, for instance. But I doubt if I can ever equal your record in potations.

HE: *[bitterly]* I can never equal your record in the soul's infidelities.

SHE: Well, do you expect my soul to be faithful when you keep hitting it with a gridiron?

HE: No, I do not expect it of you! I have about given up the hope that you will ever respond either to my ideas about household and children or about our personal relations. You seem to want as little as possible of the things that I want much. I harass you by insisting. You anger and exasperate me by retreating. We were fools not to have separated long ago.

SHE: Again! How you do repeat yourself, my dear!

HE: Yes, I am very weak. In spite of my better judgment I have loved you. But this time I mean it!

SHE: I don't believe you do. You never mean half the things you say.

HE: I do this time. This affair of yours with Hank is on my nerves. It is real spiritual infidelity. When you are interested in him you lose all interest in the household, the children and me. It is my duty to separate.

SHE: Oh, nonsense! I didn't separate from you when you were running after the widow last winter--spending hours with her every day, dining with her and leaving me alone, and telling me she was the only woman who had ever understood you.

HE: I didn't run after the widow, or any other woman except you. They ran after me.

SHE: Oh, of course! Just the same since Adam--not one of you has spirit enough to go after the apple himself! "They ran after you"--but you didn't run away very fast, did you?

HE: Why should I, when I wanted them to take possession if they could? I think I showed splendid spirit in running after you! Not more than a dozen other men have shown the same spirit. It is true, as you say, that other women understand and sympathize with me. They all do except you. I've never been able to be essentially unfaithful, more's the pity. You are abler in that regard.

SHE: I don't think so. I may have liked other people, but I never dreamed of *marrying* anyone but *you*.... No, and I never thought any of them understood me, either. I took very good care they shouldn't.

HE: Why, it was only the other day that you said Hank understood you better than I ever could. You said I was too virtuous, and that if I were worse you might see me!

SHE: As usual, you misquote me. What I said was that Hank and I were more alike, and that you are a virtuous stranger--a sort of wandering John the Baptist, preaching in the wilderness!

HE: Preachers don't do the things I do!

SHE: Oh, don't they?

HE: Well, I know I am as vicious as man can be. You would see that if you loved me. I am fully as bad as Hank.

SHE: Hank doesn't pretend to be virtuous, so perhaps you're worse. But I think you ought to make up your mind whether you're virtuous or vicious, and not assume to be both.

HE: I am both as a matter of fact, like everybody else. I am not a hypocrite. I love the virtuous and also the vicious. But I don't like to be left out in the cold when you are having an affair. When you are interested in the other, you are not in me.

SHE: Why do you pretend to fuss about lamps and such things when you are simply jealous? I call that hypocritical. I wish it were possible for a man to play fair. But what you want is to censor and control me, while you feel perfectly free to amuse yourself in every possible way.

HE: I am never jealous without cause, and you are. You object to my friendly and physical intimacies and then expect me not to be jealous of your soul's infidelities, when you lose all feeling for me. I am tired of it. It is a fundamental misunderstanding, and we ought to separate at once!

SHE: Oh, very well, if you're so keen on it. But remember, you suggest it. I never said I wanted to separate from you--if I had, I wouldn't be here now.

HE: No, because I've given all I had to you. I have nourished you with my love. You have harassed and destroyed me. I am no good because of you. You have made me work over you to the degree that I have no real life. You have enslaved me, and your method is cool aloofness. You want to keep on being cruel. You are the devil, who never really meant any harm, but who sneers at desires and never wants to satisfy. Let us separate--you are my only enemy!

SHE: Well, you know we are told to love our enemies.

HE: I have done my full duty in that respect. People we love are the only ones who can hurt us. They *are* our enemies, unless they love us in return.

SHE: "A man's enemies are those of his own household"--yes, especially if they love. You, on account of your love for me, have tyrannized over me, bothered me, badgered me, nagged me, for fifteen years. You have interfered with me, taken my time and strength, and prevented me from accomplishing great works for the good of humanity. You have crushed my soul, which longs for serenity and peace, with your perpetual complaining!

HE: Too bad. *[Indignantly.]* Perpetual complaining!

SHE: Yes, of course. But you see, my dear, I am more philosophical than you, and I recognize all this as necessity. Men and women are natural enemies, like cat and dog--only more so. They are forced to live together for a time, or this wonderful race couldn't go on. In addition, in order to have the best children, men and women of totally opposite temperaments must live together. The shock and flame of two hostile temperaments meeting is what produces fine children. Well, we have fulfilled our fate and produced our children, and they are good ones. But really--to expect also to live in peace together--we as different as fire and water, or sea and land--that's too much!

HE: If your philosophy is correct, that is another argument for separation. If we have done our job together, let's go on our ways and try to do something else separately.

SHE: Perfectly logical. Perhaps it will be best. But no divorce--that's so commonplace.

HE: Almost as commonplace as your conventional attitude toward husbands--that they are necessarily uninteresting--*mon bete de mari*--as the typical Frenchwoman of fiction says. I find divorce no more commonplace than real infidelity.

SHE: Both are matters of every day. But I see no reason for divorce unless one of the spouses wants to marry again. I shall never divorce you. But men can always have children, and so they are perpetually under the sway of the great illusion. If you want to marry again, you can divorce me.

HE: As usual, you want to see me as a brute. I don't accept your philosophy. Children are the results of love, not because of it, and love should go on. It does go on, if once there has been the right relations. It is not re-marrying or the unconscious desire for further propagation that moves me--but the eternal need of that peculiar sympathy which has never been satisfied--to die without that is failure of what most appeals to the imagination of human beings.

SHE: But that *is* precisely the great illusion. That is the unattainable that lures us on, and that will lead you, I foresee, if you leave me, into the arms of some other woman.

HE: Illusion! Precisely what *is*, you call illusion. Only there do we find Truth. And certainly I *am* bitten badly with illusion or truth, whichever it is. It is Truth to me. But I fear it may be too late. I fear the other woman is impossible.

SHE: *[pensively]* "I cannot comprehend this wild swooning desire to wallow in unbridled unity." *[He makes angry gesture, she goes on quickly.]* I was quoting your favorite philosopher. But as to being too late--no, no--you're more attractive than you ever were, and that shows your ingratitude to me, for I'm sure I have been a liberal education to you. You will easily find someone to adore you and console you for all your sufferings with me. But do be careful this time--get a good housekeeper.

HE: And *you* are more attractive than you ever were. I can see that others see that. I have been a liberal education to you, too.

SHE: Yes, a Pilgrim's Progress.

HE: I never would have seen woman, if I hadn't suffered you.

SHE: I never would have suffered man, if I hadn't seen you.

HE: You never saw me!

SHE: Alas--yes! *[With feeling.]* I saw you as something very beautiful--very fine, sensitive--with more understanding than anyone I've ever known--more feeling--I still see you that way--but from a great--distance.

HE*: [startled]* Distance?

SHE: Don't you feel how far away from one another we are?

HE: I have felt it, as you know--more and more so--that you were pushing me more and more away and seeking more and more somebody--something else. But this is the first time you have admitted feeling it.

SHE: Yes--I didn't want to admit it. But now I see it has gone very far. It is as though we were on opposite banks of a stream that grows wider--separating us more and more.

HE: Yes--

SHE: You have gone your own way, and I mine--and there is a gulf between us.

HE: Now you see what I mean--

SHE: Yes, that we ought to separate--that we *are* separated--and yet I love you.

HE: Two people may love intensely, and yet not be able to live together. It is too painful, for you, for me--

SHE: We have hurt one another too much--

HE: We have destroyed one another--we are enemies. *[Pause.]*

SHE: I don't understand it--how we have come to this--after our long life together. Have you forgotten all that? What wonderful companions we were? How gaily we took life with both hands--how we played with it and with one another! At least, we have the past.

HE: The past is bitter--because the present is bitter.

SHE: You wrong the past.

HE: The past is always judged by the present. Dante said, the worst hell is in present misery to remember former happiness--

SHE: Dante was a man and a poet, and so ungrateful to life. *[Pause with feeling]* Our past to me is wonderful and will remain so, no matter what happens--full of color and life--complete!

HE: That is because our life together has been for you an episode.

SHE: No, it is because I take life as it is, not asking too much of it--not asking that any person or any relation be perfect. But you are an idealist-- you can never be content with what it-- You have the poison, the longing for perfection in your soul.

HE: No, not for perfection, but for union. That is not demanding the impossible. Many people have it who do not love as much as we do. No work of art is right, no matter how wonderful the materials and the parts, if the whole, the unity, is not there.

SHE: That's just what I mean. You have wanted to treat our relation, and me, as clay, and model it into the form you saw in your imagination. You have been a passionate artist. But life is not a plastic material. *It* models us.

HE: You are right. I have had the egotism of the artist, directed to a material that cannot be formed. I must let go of you, and satisfy my need of union, of marriage, otherwise than with you.

SHE: Yes, but you cannot do that by seeking another woman. You would experience the same illusion--the same disillusion.

HE: How, then, can I satisfy my mystic need?

SHE: That is between you and your God--whom I know nothing about.

HE: If I could have stripped you of divinity and sought it elsewhere--in religion, in work--with the same intensity I sought it in you--we would not have needed this separation.

SHE: And we should have been very happy together!

HE: Yes--as interesting changers.

SHE: Exactly. The only sensible way for two fully grown people to be together--and that is wonderful, too--think! To have lived together for fifteen years and never to have bored one another! To be still for one another the most interesting persons in the world! How many married people can say that? I've never *bored* you, have I, Deacon?

HE: You have harassed, plagued, maddened, tortured me! Bored me? No, never, you bewitching devil! *[Moving toward her.]*

SHE: I've always adored the poet and mystic in you, though you've almost driven me crazy, you Man of God!

HE: I've always adored the woman in you, the mysterious, the beckoning and flying, that I cannot possess!

SHE: Can't you forget God for a while, and come away with me?

HE: Yes, darling; after all, you're one of God's creatures!

SHE: Faithful to the end! A truce then, shall it be? *[Opening her arms.]* An armed truce?

HE: *[seizing her]* Yes, in a trice! *[She laughs.]*

CURTAIN

THE PRETENTIOUS YOUNG LADIES

Molière

CHARACTERS:

LA GRANGE, a repulsed lover
DU CROISY, a repulsed lover
GORGIBUS, a good citizen
THE MARQUIS DE MASCARILLE, valet to La Grange
THE VISCOUNT JODELET, valet to Du Croisy
ALMANZOR, footman to the pretentious ladies
TWO CHAIRMEN
MUSICIANS
MADELON, daughter to Gorgibus; a pretentious young lady
CATHOS: niece to Gorgibus; a pretentious young lady
MAROTTE, maid to the pretentious young ladies
LUCILE, a female neighbor
CÉLIMÈNE, a female neighbor

SCENE:

House of Gorgibus; Paris.

SCENE I

LA GRANGE, DU CROISY.

DU CROISY: Mr. La Grange.

LA GRANGE: What?

DU CROISY: Look at me for a moment without laughing.

LA GRANGE: Well?

DU CROISY: What do you say of our visit? Are you quite pleased with it?

LA GRANGE: Do you think either of us has any reason to be so?

DU CROISY: Not at all, to say the truth.

LA GRANGE: As for me, I must acknowledge I was quite shocked at it. Pray now, did ever anybody see a couple of country wenches giving themselves more ridiculous airs, or two men treated with more contempt than we were? They could hardly make up their mind to order chairs for us. I never saw such whispering as there was between them; such yawning, such rubbing of the eyes, and asking so often what o'clock it was. Did they answer anything else but "yes," or "no," to what we said to them? In short, do you not agree with me that if we had been the meanest persons in the world, we could not have been treated worse?

DU CROISY: You seem to take it greatly to heart.

LA GRANGE: No doubt I do; so much so, that I am resolved to be revenged on them for their impertinence. I know well enough why they despise us. Affectation has not alone infected Paris, but has also spread into the country, and our ridiculous damsels have sucked in their share of it. In a word, they are a strange medley of coquetry and affectation. I plainly see what kind of persons will be well received by them; if you will take my advice, we will play them such a trick as shall show them their folly, and teach them to distinguish a little better the people they have to deal with.

DU CROISY: How can you do this?

LA GRANGE: I have a certain valet, named Mascarille, who, in the opinion of many people, passes for a kind of wit; for nothing now-a-days is easier than to acquire such a reputation. He is an extraordinary fellow, who has taken it into his head to ape a person of quality. He usually prides himself on his gallantry and his poetry, and despises so much the other servants that he calls them brutes.

DU CROISY: What do you mean to do with him?

LA GRANGE: What do I mean to do with him? He must . . . but first, let us be gone.

SCENE II

GORGIBUS, DU CROISY, LA GRANGE.

GORGIBUS: Well, gentlemen, you have seen my niece and my daughter. How are matters going on? What is the result of your visit?

LA GRANGE: They will tell you this better than we can. All we say is that we thank you for the favor you have done us, and remain your most humble servants.

GORGIBUS: *[Alone.]* Hoity-toity! Methinks they go away dissatisfied. What can be the meaning of this? I must find out. Within there!

SCENE III

GORGIBUS, MAROTTE.

MAROTTE: Did you call, sir?

GORGIBUS: Where are your mistresses?

MAROTTE: In their room.

GORGIBUS: What are they doing there?

MAROTTE: Making lip salve.

GORGIBUS: There is no end of their salves. Bid them come down. *[Alone.]* These hussies with their salves have, I think, a mind to ruin me. Everywhere in the house I see nothing but whites of eggs, lac virginal, and a thousand other fooleries I am not acquainted with. Since we have been here they have employed the lard of a dozen hogs at least, and four servants might live every day on the sheep's trotters they use.

SCENE IV

MADELON, CATHOS, GORGIBUS.

GORGIBUS: Truly there is great need to spend so much money to grease your faces. Pray tell me, what have you done to those gentlemen, that I saw them go away with so much coldness. Did I not order you to receive them as persons whom I intended for your husbands?

MADELON: Dear father, what consideration do you wish us to entertain for the irregular behavior of these people?

CATHOS: How can a woman of ever so little understanding, uncle, reconcile herself to such individuals?

GORGIBUS: What fault have you to find with them?

MADELON: Theirs is a fine gallantry, indeed. Would you believe it? They began with proposing marriage to us.

GORGIBUS: What would you have them begin with--with a proposal to keep you as mistresses? Is not their proposal a compliment to both of you, as well as to me? Can anything be more polite than this? And do they not prove the honesty of their intentions by wishing to enter these holy bonds?

MADELON: O, father! Nothing can be more vulgar than what you have just said. I am ashamed to hear you talk in such a manner; you should take some lessons in the elegant way of looking at things.

GORGIBUS: I care neither for elegant ways nor for airs. I tell you marriage is a holy and sacred affair; to begin with that is to act like honest people.

MADELON: Good Heavens! If everybody was like you a love-story would soon be over. What a fine thing it would have been if Cyrus had immediately espoused Mandane, and if Aronce had been married at once to Clélie.

GORGIBUS: What is she jabbering about?

MADELON: Here is my cousin, father, who will tell as well as I that matrimony ought never to happen till after other adventures. A lover, to be agreeable, must understand how to utter fine sentiments, to breathe soft, tender, and passionate vows; his courtship must be according to the rules. In the first place, he should behold the fair one of whom he becomes enamored either at a place of worship, or when out walking, or at some public ceremony; or else he should be introduced to her by a relative or a friend, as if by chance, and when he leaves her he should appear in a pensive and melancholy mood. For some time he should conceal his passion from the object of his love, but pay her several visits, in every one of which he ought to introduce some gallant subject to exercise the wits of all the company. When the day comes to make his declarations--which generally should be contrived in some shady garden-walk while the company is at a distance--it should be quickly followed by anger, which is shown by our blushing, and which, for a while, banishes the lover from our presence. He finds afterwards means to pacify us, to accustom us gradually to hear him depict his passion, and to draw from us that confession which causes us so much pain. After that come the adventures, the rivals who thwart mutual inclination, the persecutions of fathers, the jealousies arising without any foundation, complaints, despair, running away with, and its consequences. Thus things are carried on in fashionable life, and veritable gallantry cannot dispense with these forms. But to come out point-blank with a proposal of marriage--to make no love but with a marriage-contract, and begin a novel at the wrong end! Once more, father, nothing can be more tradesman like, and the mere thought of it makes me sick at heart.

GORGIBUS: What deuced nonsense is all this? That is high-flown language with a vengeance!

CATHOS: Indeed, uncle, my cousin hits the nail on the head. How can we receive kindly those who are so awkward in gallantry? I could lay a wager they have not even seen a map of the country of *Tenderness*, and that *Love-letters, Trifling attentions, Polite epistles,* and *Sprightly verses,* are regions to them unknown. Do you not see that the whole person shows it, and that their external appearance is not such as to give at first sight a good opinion of them. To come and pay a visit to the object of their love with a leg without any ornaments, a hat without any feathers, a head with its locks not artistically arranged, and a coat that suffers from a paucity of ribbons.

Heavens! What lovers are these! What stinginess in dress! What barrenness of conversation! It is not to be allowed; it is not to be borne. I also observed that their ruffs were not made by the fashionable milliner, and that their breeches were not big enough by more than half-a-foot.

GORGIBUS: I think they are both mad, nor can I understand anything of this gibberish. Cathos, and you Madelon . . .

MADELON: Pray, father, do not use those strange names, and call us by some other.

GORGIBUS: What do you mean by those strange names? Are they not the names your godfathers and godmothers gave you?

MADELON: Good Heavens! How vulgar you are! I confess I wonder you could possibly be the father of such an intelligent girl as I am. Did ever anybody in genteel style talk of Cathos or Madelon? And must you not admit that either of these names would be sufficient to disgrace the finest novel in the world?

CATHOS: It is true, uncle, an ear rather delicate suffers extremely at hearing these words pronounced, and the name of Polixena, which my cousin has chosen, and that of Amintha, which I took, possesses a charm, which you must needs acknowledge.

GORGIBUS: Hearken; one word will suffice. I do not allow you to take any other names than those that were given you by your godfathers and godmothers; and as for those gentlemen we are speaking about, I know their families and fortunes, and am determined they shall be your husbands. I am tired of having you upon my hands. Looking after a couple of girls is rather too weighty a charge for a man of my years.

CATHOS: As for me, uncle, all I can say is that I think marriage a very shocking business. How can one endure the thought of lying by the side of a man, who is really naked?

MADELON: Give us leave to take breath for a short time among the fashionable world of Paris, where we are but just arrived. Allow us to prepare at our leisure the groundwork of our novel, and do not hurry on the conclusion too abruptly.

GORGIBUS: *[Aside.]* I cannot doubt it any longer; they are completely mad. *[Aloud.]* Once more, I tell you, I understand nothing of all this gibberish; I will be master, and to cut short all kinds of arguments, either you shall both be married shortly, or, upon my word, you shall be nuns; that I swear.

SCENE V

CATHOS, MADELON.

CATHOS: Good Heavens, my dear, how deeply is your father still immersed in material things! How dense is his understanding, and what gloom overcasts his soul!

MADELON: What can I do, my dear? I am ashamed of him. I can hardly persuade myself I am indeed his daughter; I believe that an accident, some time or other, will discover me to be of a more illustrious descent.

CATHOS: I believe it; really, it is very likely; as for me, when I consider myself . . .

SCENE VI

CATHOS, MADELON, MAROTTE.

MAROTTE: Here is a footman asks if you are at home, and says his master is coming to see you.

MADELON: Learn, you dunce, to express yourself a little less vulgarly. Say, here is a necessary evil inquiring if it is commodious for you to become visible.

MAROTTE: I do not understand Latin, and have not learned philosophy out of Cyrus, as you have done.

MADELON: Impertinent creature! How can this be borne! And who is this footman's master?

MAROTTE: He told me it was the Marquis de Mascarille.

MADELON: Ah, my dear! A marquis! A marquis! Well, go and tell him we are visible. This is certainly some wit who has heard of us.

CATHOS: Undoubtedly, my dear.

MADELON: We had better receive him here in this parlor than in our room. Let us at least arrange our hair a little and maintain our reputation. Come in quickly, and reach us the Counselor of the Graces.

MAROTTE: Upon my word, I do not know what sort of a beast that is; you must speak like a Christian if you would have me know your meaning.

CATHOS: Bring us the looking-glass, you blockhead! And take care not to contaminate its brightness by the communication of your image.

SCENE VII

MASCARILLE, TWO CHAIRMEN.

MASCARILLE: Stop, chairman, stop. Easy does it! Easy, easy! I think these boobies intend to break me to pieces by bumping me against the walls and the pavement.

1ST CHAIRMAN: Ay, marry, because the gate is narrow and you would make us bring you in here.

MASCARILLE: To be sure, you rascals! Would you have me expose the fullness of my plumes to the inclemency of the rainy season, and let the mud receive the impression of my shoes? Be gone; take away your chair.

2ND CHAIRMAN: Then please to pay us, sir.

MASCARILLE: What?

2ND CHAIRMAN: Sir, please to give us our money, I say.

MASCARILLE: [*Giving him a box on the ear.*] What, scoundrel, to ask money from a person of my rank!

2ND CHAIRMAN: Is this the way poor people are to be paid? Will your rank get us dinner?

MASCARILLE: Ha, ha! I shall teach you to keep your right place. Those low fellows dare to make fun of me!

1ST CHAIRMAN: *[Taking up the poles of his chair.]* Come, pay us quickly.

MASCARILLE: What?

1ST CHAIRMAN: I mean to have my money at once.

MASCARILLE: That is a sensible fellow.

1ST CHAIRMAN: Make haste, then.

MASCARILLE: Ay, you speak properly, but the other is a scoundrel who does not know what he says. There, are you satisfied?

1ST CHAIRMAN: No, I am not satisfied; you boxed my friend's ears. *[Holding up his pole.]*

MASCARILLE: Gently; there is something for the box on the ear. People may get anything from me when they go about it in the right way. Go now, but come and fetch me by and by to carry me to the Louvre to the *petit coucher.*

[NOTE: Louis XIV, and several other Kings of France, received their courtiers when rising or going to bed. This was called lever and coucher. The lever as well as the coucher was divided into petit and grand. All persons received at court had a right to come to the grand lever and coucher, but only certain noblemen of high rank and the princess of the royal blood could remain at the petit lever and coucher, which was the time between the king putting on either a day or night shirt, and the time he went to bed or was fully dressed. The highest person of rank always claimed the right of handing to the king his shirt.]

SCENE VIII

MAROTTE, MASCARILLE.

MAROTTE: Sir, my mistresses will come immediately.

MASCARILLE: Let them not hurry themselves; I am very comfortable here, and can wait.

MAROTTE: Here they come.

SCENE IX

MADELON, CATHOS, MASCARILLE, ALMANZOR.

MASCARILLE: *[After having bowed to them.]* Ladies, no doubt you will be surprised at the boldness of my visit, but your reputation has drawn this disagreeable affair upon you; merit has for me such potent charms, that I run everywhere after it.

MADELON: If you pursue merit you should not come to us.

CATHOS: If you find merit amongst us, you must have brought it hither yourself.

MASCARILLE: Ah! I protest against these words. When fame mentioned your deserts it spoke the truth, and you are going to make *pic, repic*, and *capot* all the gallants from Paris.

MADELON: Your complaisance goes a little too far in the liberality of its praises, and my cousin and I must take credit not to give too much credit to your sweet adulation.

CATHOS: My dear, we should call for chairs.

MADELON: Almanzor!

ALMANZOR: Madam.

MADELON: Convey to us hither, instantly, the conveniences of conversation.

MASCARILLE: But am I safe here? *[Exit ALMANZOR.]*

CATHOS: What is it you fear?

MASCARILLE: Some larceny of my heart; some massacre of liberty. I behold here a pair of eyes that seem to be very naughty boys, that insult liberty, and use a heart most barbarously. Why the deuce do they put themselves on their guard, in order to kill any one who comes near them? Upon my word! I mistrust them; I shall either scamper away, or expect very good security that they do me no mischief.

MADELON: My dear, what a charming facetiousness he has!

CATHOS: I see, indeed, he is an Amilcar.

MADELON: Fear nothing, our eyes have no wicked designs, and your heart may rest in peace, fully assured of their innocence.

CATHOS: But, pray, Sir, be not inexorable to the easy chair, which, for this last quarter of an hour, has held out its arms towards you; yield to its desire of embracing you.

MASCARILLE: *[After having combed himself and adjusted the rolls of his stockings.]* Well, ladies, and what do you think of Paris?

MADELON: Alas! What can we think of it? It would be the very antipodes of reason not to confess that Paris is the grand cabinet of marvels, the centre of good taste, wit, and gallantry.

MASCARILLE: As for me, I maintain that, out of Paris, there is no salvation for the polite world.

CATHOS: Most assuredly.

MASCARILLE: Paris is somewhat muddy; but then we have sedan chairs.

MADELON: To be sure; a sedan chair is a wonderful protection against the insults of mud and bad weather.

MASCARILLE: I am sure you receive many visits. What great wit belongs to your company?

MADELON: Alas! We are not yet known, but we are in the way of being so; for a lady of our acquaintance has promised us to bring all the gentlemen who have written for the *Miscellanies of Select Poetry*.

CATHOS: And certain others, whom, we have been told, are likewise the sovereign arbiters of all that is handsome.

MASCARILLE: I can manage this for you better than any one; they all visit me; and I may say that I never rise without having half-a-dozen wits at my levee.

MADELON: Good Heavens! You will place us under the greatest obligation if you will do us the kindness; for, in short, we must make the acquaintance of all those gentlemen if we wish to belong to the fashion. They are the persons who can make or unmake a reputation at Paris; you know that there are some, whose visits alone are sufficient to start the report that you are a *Connaisseuse*, though there should be no reason for it. As for me, what I value particularly is that by means of these ingenious visits, we learn a hundred things which we ought necessarily to know, and which are the quintessence of wit. Through them we hear the scandal of the day, or whatever niceties are going on in prose or verse. We know, at the right time, that Mr. So-and-so has written the finest piece in the world on such a subject; that Mrs. So-and-so has adapted words to such a tune; that a certain gentleman has written a madrigal upon a favor shown to him; another stanzas upon a fair one who betrayed him; Mr. Such-a-one wrote a couplet of six lines yesterday evening to Miss Such-a-one, to which she returned him an answer this morning at eight o'clock; such an author is engaged on such a subject; this writer is busy with the third volume of his novel; that one is putting his works to press. Those things procure you consideration in every society, and if people are ignorant of them, I would not give one pinch of snuff for all the wit they may have.

CATHOS: Indeed, I think it the height of ridicule for anyone who possesses the slightest claim to be called clever not to know even the smallest couplet that is made every day; as for me, I should be very much ashamed if any one should ask me my opinion about something new, and I had not seen it.

MASCARILLE: It is really a shame not to know from the very first all that is going on; but do not give yourself any farther trouble, I will establish an academy of wits at your house, and I give you my word that not a single line of poetry shall be written in Paris, but what you shall be able to say by heart before anybody else. As for me, such as you see me, I amuse myself in that way when I am in the humor, and you may find handed about in the fashionable assemblies of Paris two hundred songs, as many sonnets, four hundred epigrams, and more than a thousand madrigals all made by me, without counting riddles and portraits.

MADELON: I must admit that I dote upon portraits; I think there is nothing more gallant.

MASCARILLE: Portraits are difficult, and call for great wit; you shall see some of mine that will not displease you.

CATHOS: As for me, I am awfully fond of riddles.

MASCARILLE: They exercise the intelligence; I have already written four of them this morning, which I will give you to guess.

MADELON: Madrigals are pretty enough when they are neatly turned.

MASCARILLE: This is my special talent; I am at present engaged in turning the whole Roman history into madrigals.

MADELON: Goodness gracious! That will certainly be superlatively fine; I should like to have one copy at least, if you think of publishing it.

MASCARILLE: I promise you each a copy, bound in the handsomest manner. It does not become a man of my rank to scribble, but I do it only to serve the publishers, who are always bothering me.

MADELON: I fancy it must be a delightful thing to see one's self in print.

MASCARILLE: Undoubtedly; but, by the by, I must repeat to you some extempore verses I made yesterday at the house of a certain duchess, an acquaintance of mine. I am deuced clever at extempore verses.

CATHOS: Extempore verses are certainly the very touchstone of genius.

MASCARILLE: Listen then.

MADELON: We are all ears.

MASCARILLE: *Oh! Oh! Quite without heed was I,*
As harmless you I chanced to spy,
Slyly your eyes
My heart surprise,
Stop thief! Stop thief! Stop thief I cry!

CATHOS: Good Heavens! This is carried to the utmost pitch of gallantry.

MASCARILLE: Everything I do shows it is done by a gentleman; there is nothing of the pedant about my effusions.

MADELON: They are more than two thousand miles removed from that.

MASCARILLE: Did you observe the beginning, *Oh! Oh?* There is something original in that *Oh! Oh!* like a man who all of a sudden thinks about something, *Oh! Oh!* Taken by surprise as it were, *Oh! Oh!*

MADELON: Yes, I think that *Oh! Oh!* admirable.

MASCARILLE: It seems a mere nothing.

CATHOS: Good Heavens! How can you say so? It is one of these things that are perfectly invaluable.

MADELON: No doubt on it; I would rather have written that *Oh! Oh!* than an epic poem.

MASCARILLE: Egad, you have good taste.

MADELON: Tolerably; none of the worst, I believe.

MASCARILLE: But do you not also admire *quite without heed was I? quite without heed was I,* that is, I did not pay attention to anything; a natural way of speaking, *quite without heed was I, of no harm thinking,* that is, as I was going along, innocently, without malice, like a poor sheep, *you I chanced to spy,* that is to say, I amused myself with looking at you, with observing you, with contemplating you. *Slyly your eyes . . .* What do you think of that word *slyly*--is it not well chosen?

CATHOS: Extremely so.

MASCARILLE: *Slyly,* stealthily; just like a cat watching a mouse--*slyly.*

MADELON: Nothing can be better.

MASCARILLE: *My heart surprise,* that is, carries it away from me, robs me of it. *Stop thief! Stop thief! Stop thief!* Would you not think a man were shouting and running after a thief to catch him? *Stop thief! Stop thief! Stop thief!*

MADELON: I must admit the turn is witty and sprightly.

MASCARILLE: I will sing you the tune I made of it.

CATHOS: Have you learned music?

MASCARILLE: I? Not at all.

CATHOS: How can you make a tune then?

MASCARILLE: People of rank know everything without ever having learned anything.

MADELON: His lordship is quite in the right, my dear.

MASCARILLE: Listen if you like the tune: *hem, hem, la, la*. The inclemency of the season has greatly injured the delicacy of my voice; but no matter, it is in a free and easy way. *[He sings.] Oh! Oh! Quite without heed was I*, etc...

CATHOS: What a passion there breathes in this music. It is enough to make one die away with delight!

MADELON: There is something plaintive in it.

MASCARILLE: Do you not think that the air perfectly well expresses the sentiment, *stop thief, stop thief*? And then as if some one cried out very loud, *stop, stop, stop, stop, stop, stop thief!* Then all at once like a person out of breath, *Stop thief!*

MADELON: This is to understand the perfection of things, the grand perfection, the perfection of perfections. I declare it is altogether a wonderful performance. I am quite enchanted with the air and the words.

CATHOS: I never yet met anything so excellent.

MASCARILLE: All that I do comes naturally to me; it is without study.

MADELON: Nature has treated you like a very fond mother; you are her darling child.

MASCARILLE: How do you pass away the time, ladies?

CATHOS: With nothing at all.

MADELON: Until now we have lived in a terrible dearth of amusements.

MASCARILLE: I am at your service to attend you to the play, one of those days, if you will permit me. Indeed, a new comedy is to be acted which I should be very glad we might see together.

MADELON: There is no refusing you anything.

MASCARILLE: But I beg of you to applaud it well, when we shall be there; for I have promised to give a helping hand to the piece. The author called upon me this very morning to beg me so to do. It is the custom for authors to come and read their new plays to people of rank, that they may induce us to improve them and give them a reputation. I leave you to imagine if, when we say anything, the pit dares contradict us. As for me, I am very punctual in these things, and when I have made a promise to a poet, I always call out "Bravo" before the candles are lighted.

MADELON: Do not say another word; Paris is an admirable place. A hundred things happen every day which people in the country, however clever they may be, have no idea of.

CATHOS: Since you have told us, we shall consider it our duty to cry up lustily every word that is said.

MASCARILLE: I do not know whether I am deceived, but you look as if you had written some play yourself.

MADELON: Eh! There may be something in what you say.

MASCARILLE: Ah! Upon my word, we must see it. Between ourselves, I have written one which I intend to have brought out.

CATHOS: Ay! To what company do you mean to give it?

MASCARILLE: That is a very nice question, indeed. To the actors of the Hôtel de Bourgogne; they alone can bring things into good repute; the rest are ignorant creatures who recite their parts just as people speak in everyday life; they do not understand to mouth the verses, or to pause at a beautiful passage; how can it be known where the fine lines are, if an actor does not stop at them, and thereby tell you to applaud heartily?

CATHOS: Indeed! That is one way of making an audience feel the beauties of any work; things are only prized when they are well set off.

MASCARILLE: What do you think of my top-knot, sword-knot, and rosettes? Do you find they harmonize with my coat?

CATHOS: Perfectly.

MASCARILLE: Do you think the ribbon well chosen?

MADELON: Furiously well. It is real Perdrigeon.

MASCARILLE: What do you say of my rolls?

MADELON: They look very fashionable.

MASCARILLE: I may at least boast that they are a quarter of a yard wider than any that have been made.

MADELON: I must own I never saw the elegance of dress carried farther.

MASCARILLE: Please to fasten the reflection of your smelling faculty upon these gloves.

MADELON: They smell awfully fine.

CATHOS: I never inhaled a more delicious perfume.

MASCARILLE: And this? *[He gives them his powdered wig to smell.]*

MADELON: It has the true quality odor; it titillates the nerves of the upper region most deliciously.

MASCARILLE: You say nothing of my feathers. How do you like them?

CATHOS: They are frightfully beautiful.

MASCARILLE: Do you know that every single one of them cost me a Louis-d'or? But it is my hobby to have generally everything of the very best.

MADELON: I assure you that you and I sympathize. I am furiously particular in everything I wear; I cannot endure even stockings, unless they are bought at a fashionable shop.

MASCARILLE: *[Crying out suddenly.]* O! O! O! Gently. Damme, ladies, you use me very ill; I have reason to complain of your behavior; it is not fair.

CATHOS: What is the matter with you?

MASCARILLE: What! Two at once against my heart! To attack me thus right and left! Ha! This is contrary to the law of nations, the combat is too unequal, and I must cry out, "Murder!"

CATHOS: Well, he does say things in a peculiar way.

MADELON: He is a consummate wit.

CATHOS: You are more afraid than hurt, and your heart cries out before it is even wounded.

MASCARILLE: The devil it does! It is wounded all over from head to foot.

SCENE X

CATHOS, MADELON, MASCARILLE, MAROTTE.

MAROTTE: Madam, somebody asks to see you.

MADELON: Who!

MAROTTE: The Viscount de Jodelet.

MASCARILLE: The Viscount de Jodelet?

MAROTTE: Yes, sir.

CATHOS: Do you know him?

MASCARILLE: He is my most intimate friend.

MADELON: Show him in immediately.

MASCARILLE: We have not seen each other for some time; I am delighted to meet him.

CATHOS: Here he comes.

SCENE XI

CATHOS, MADELON, JODELET, MASCARILLE, MAROTTE, ALMANZOR.

MASCARILLE: Ah, Viscount!

JODELET: Ah, Marquis! *[Embracing each other.]*

MASCARILLE: How glad I am to meet you!

JODELET: How happy I am to see you here.

MASCARILLE: Embrace me once more, I pray you.

MADELON: *[To CATHOS.]* My dearest, we begin to be known; people of fashion find the way to our house.

MASCARILLE: Ladies, allow me to introduce this gentleman to you. Upon my word, he deserves the honor of your acquaintance.

JODELET: It is but just we should come and pay you what we owe; your charms demand their lordly rights from all sorts of people.

MADELON: You carry your civilities to the utmost confines of flattery.

CATHOS: This day ought to be marked in our diary as a red-letter day.

MADELON: *[To ALMANZOR.]* Come, boy, must you always be told things over and over again? Do you not observe there must be an additional chair?

MASCARILLE: You must not be astonished to see the Viscount thus; he has but just recovered from an illness, which, as you perceive, has made him so pale.

JODELET: The consequence of continual attendance at court and the fatigues of war.

MASCARILLE: Do you know, ladies, that in the Viscount you behold one of the heroes of the age. He is a very valiant man.

JODELET: Marquis, you are not inferior to me; we also know what you can do.

MASCARILLE: It is true we have seen one another at work when there was need for it.

JODELET: And in places where it was hot.

MASCARILLE: *[Looking at CATHOS and MADELON.]* Ay, but not so hot as here. Ha, ha, ha!

JODELET: We became acquainted in the army; the first time we saw each other he commanded a regiment of horse aboard the galleys of Malta.

MASCARILLE: True, but for all that you were in the service before me; I remember that I was but a young officer when you commanded two thousand horse.

JODELET: War is a fine thing; but, upon my word, the court does not properly reward men of merit like us.

MASCARILLE: That is the reason I intend to hang up my sword.

CATHOS: As for me, I have a tremendous liking for gentlemen of the army.

MADELON: I love them, too; but I like bravery seasoned with wit.

MASCARILLE: Do you remember, Viscount, our taking that half-moon from the enemy at the siege of Arras?

JODELET: What do you mean by half-moon? It was a complete full moon.

MASCARILLE: I believe you are right.

JODELET: Upon my word, I ought to remember it very well. I was wounded in the leg by a hand-grenade, of which I still carry the marks. Pray, feel it, you can perceive what sort of wound it was.

CATHOS: *[Putting her hand to the place.]* The scar is really large.

MASCARILLE: Give me your hand for a moment, and feel this; there, just at the back of my head. Do you feel it?

MADELON: Ay, I feel something.

MASCARILLE: A musket shot which I received the last campaign I served in.

JODELET: *[Unbuttoning his breast.]* Here is a wound which went quite through me at the attack of Gravelines.

MASCARILLE: *[Putting his hand upon the button of his breeches.]* I am going to show you a tremendous wound.

MADELON: There is no occasion for it, we believe it without seeing it.

MASCARILLE: They are honor's marks, that show what a man is made of.

CATHOS: We have not the least doubt of the valor of you both.

MASCARILLE: Viscount, is your coach waiting?

JODELET: Why?

MASCARILLE: We shall give these ladies an airing, and offer them a collation.

MADELON: We cannot go out today.

MASCARILLE: Let us send for musicians then, and have a dance.

JODELET: Upon my word, that is a happy thought.

MADELON: With all our hearts, but we must have some additional company.

MASCARILLE: So ho! Champagne, Picard, Bourguignon, Cascaret, Basque, La Verdure, Lorrain, Provençal, La Violette. I wish the deuce took all these footmen! I do not think there is a gentleman in France worse served than I am! These rascals are always out of the way.

MADELON: Almanzor, tell the servants of my lord marquis to go and fetch the musicians, and ask some of the gentlemen and ladies hereabouts to come and people the solitude of our ball. *[Exit ALMANZOR.]*

MASCARILLE: What do you say of those eyes?

JODELET: Why, Marquis, what do you think of them yourself?

MASCARILLE: I? I say that our liberty will have much difficulty to get away from here scot free. At least mine has suffered most violent attacks; my heart hangs by a simple thread.

MADELON: How natural is all he says! He gives to things a most agreeable turn.

CATHOS: He must really spend a tremendous deal of wit.

MASCARILLE: To show you that I am in earnest, I shall make some extempore verses upon my passion. *[Seems to think.]*

CATHOS: O! I beseech you by all that I hold sacred, let us hear something made upon us.

JODELET: I should be glad to do so too, but the quantity of blood that has been taken from me lately, has greatly exhausted my poetic vein.

MASCARILLE: Deuce take it! I always make the first verse well, but I find the others more difficult. Upon my word, this is too short a time; but I will make you some extempore verses at my leisure, which you shall think the finest in the world.

JODELET: He is devilish witty.

MADELON: He--his wit is so gallant and well expressed.

MASCARILLE: Viscount, tell me, when did you see the Countess last?

JODELET: I have not paid her a visit these three weeks.

MASCARILLE: Do you know that the duke came to see me this morning; he would fain have taken me into the country to hunt a stag with him?

MADELON: Here come our friends.

SCENE XII

LUCILE, CÉLIMÈNE, CATHOS, MADELON, MASCARILLE, JODELET, MAROTTE, ALMANZOR, AND MUSICIANS.

MADELON: Lawk! My dears, we beg your pardon. These gentlemen had a fancy to put life into our heels; we sent for you to fill up the void of our assembly.

LUCILE: We are certainly much obliged to you for doing so.

MASCARILLE: This is a kind of extempore ball, ladies, but one of these days we shall give you one in form. Have the musicians come?

ALMANZOR: Yes, sir, they are here.

CATHOS: Come then, my dears, take your places.

MASCARILLE: *[Dancing by himself and singing.]* La, la, la, la, la, la, la, la.

MADELON: What a very elegant shape he has.

CATHOS: He looks as if he were a first-rate dancer.

MASCARILLE: *[Taking out MADELON to dance.]* My freedom will dance a Couranto as well as my feet. Play in time, musicians, in time. O what ignorant wretches! There is no dancing with them. The devil take you all, can you not play in time? La, la, la, la, la, la, la, la? Steady, you country-scrapers.

JODELET: *[Dancing also.]* Hold, do not play so fast. I have but just recovered from an illness.

SCENE XIII

DU CROISY, LA GRANGE, CATHOS, MADELON, LUCILE, CÉLIMÈNE, JODELET, MASCARILLE, MAROTTE, AND MUSICIANS.

LA GRANGE: *[With a stick in his hand.]* Ah! ah! scoundrels, what are you doing here? We have been looking for you these three hours. *[He beats MASCARILLE.]*

MASCARILLE: Oh! Oh! Oh! You did not tell me that blows should be dealt about.

JODELET: *[Who is also beaten.]* Oh! Oh! Oh!

LA GRANGE: It becomes you well, you rascal, to pretend to be a man of rank.

DU CROISY: This will teach you to know yourself.

SCENE XIV

CATHOS, MADELON, LUCILE, CÉLIMÈNE, JODELET, MASCARILLE, MAROTTE, AND MUSICIANS.

MADELON: What is the meaning of this?

JODELET: It is a wager.

CATHOS: What, allow yourselves to be beaten thus?

MASCARILLE: Good Heavens! I did not wish to appear to take any notice of it; because I am naturally very violent, and should have flown into a passion.

MADELON: To suffer an insult like that in our presence!

MASCARILLE: It is nothing. Let us not leave off. We have known one another for a long time, and among friends one ought not to be so quickly offended for such a trifle.

SCENE XV

DU CROISY, LA GRANGE, CATHOS, MADELON, LUCILE, CÉLIMÈNE, JODELET, MASCARILLE, MAROTTE, AND MUSICIANS.

LA GRANGE: Upon my word, rascals, you shall not laugh at us, I promise you. Come in, you there. *[Three or four men enter.]*

MADELON: What means this impudence to come and disturb us in our own house?

DU CROISY: What, ladies, shall we allow our footmen to be received better than ourselves? Shall they come to make love to you at our expense, and even give a ball in your honor?

MADELON: Your footmen?

LA GRANGE: Yes, our footmen; and you must give me leave to say that it is not acting either handsome or honest to spoil them for us, as you do.

MADELON: O Heaven! What insolence!

LA GRANGE: But they shall not have the advantage of our clothes to dazzle your eyes. Upon my word, if you are resolved to like them, it shall be for their handsome looks only. Quick, let them be stripped immediately.

JODELET: Farewell, a long farewell to all our fine clothes.

MASCARILLE: The marquisate and viscountship are at an end.

DU CROISY: Ah! Ah! You knaves, you have the impudence to become our rivals. I assure you, you must go somewhere else to borrow finery to make yourselves agreeable to your mistresses.

LA GRANGE: It is too much to supplant us, and that with our own clothes.

MASCARILLE: O fortune, how fickle you are!

DU CROISY: Quick, pull off everything from them.

LA GRANGE: Make haste and take away all these clothes. Now, ladies, in their present condition you may continue your amours with them as long as you please; we leave you perfectly free; this gentleman and I declare solemnly that we shall not be in the least degree jealous.

SCENE XVI

CATHOS, MADELON, JODELET, MASCARILLE, AND MUSICIANS.

CATHOS: What a confusion!

MADELON: I am nearly bursting with vexation.

1ST MUSICIAN: *[To MASCARILLE.]* What is the meaning of this? Who is to pay us?

MASCARILLE: Ask my lord the viscount.

1ST MUSICIAN: *[To JODELET.]* Who is to give us our money?

JODELET: Ask my lord the marquis.

SCENE XVII

GORGIBUS, MADELON, CATHOS, JODELET, MASCARILLE, AND MUSICIANS.

GORGIBUS: Ah! You hussies, you have put us in a nice pickle, by what I can see; I have heard about your fine goings on from those two gentlemen who just left.

MADELON: Ah, father! They have played us a cruel trick.

GORGIBUS: Yes, it is a cruel trick, but you may thank your own impertinence for it, you jades. They have revenged themselves for the way you treated them; and yet, unhappy man that I am, I must put up with this affront.

MADELON: Ah! I swear we will be revenged, or I shall die in the attempt. And you, rascals, dare you remain here after your insolence?

MASCARILLE: Do you treat a marquis in this manner? This is the way of the world; the least misfortune causes us to be slighted by those who before caressed us. Come along, brother, let us go and seek our fortune somewhere else; I perceive they love nothing here but outward show, and have no regard for worth unadorned. *[The both leave.]*

SCENE XVIII

GORGIBUS, MADELON, CATHOS, AND MUSICIANS.

1ST MUSICIAN: Sir, as they have not paid us, we expect you to do so, for it was in this house we played.

GORGIBUS: *[Beating them.]* Yes, yes, I shall satisfy you; this is the coin I will pay you in. As for you, you sluts, I do not know why I should not serve you in the same way; we shall become the common talk and laughing-stock of everybody; this is what you have brought upon yourselves by your fooleries. Out of my sight and hide yourselves, you jades; go and hide yourselves forever. *[Alone.]* And you, that are the cause of their folly, you stupid trash, mischievous amusements for idle minds, you novels, verses, songs, sonnets, and sonatas, the devil take you all.

CURTAIN

FOURTEEN

Alice Gerstenberg

CHARACTERS:

MRS. HORACE PRINGLE: A woman of fashion.
ELAINE: Her debutante daughter.
DUNHAM: The butler or maid.

[SCENE: The dining-room of a New York residence. A long table running from left to right, with a chair at each end and six chairs on each side, is set elaborately for fourteen. DUNHAM, the butler, is hovering over the table to give it a few finishing touches as MRS. PRINGLE comes in. She is a woman of fashion, handsome, and wears a very lovely evening gown. She is rather excitable in temperament but withal capable and executive, vivacious and humorously charming. She enters in haste carrying a corsage bouquet of flowers and the empty box of paper from which she has unwrapped them.]

MRS. PRINGLE: Dunham, I've just had word from Mr. Harper that he was called away to the bedside of a friend who is very ill. He sent me these flowers -- it's a good thing he *did*. I don't approve of young men refusing dinner invitations at the very last minute.

DUNHAM: *[Relieving her.]* I'll take the box and paper, Mrs. Pringle.

MRS. PRINGLE: *[Looking at the table anxiously and then at her watch.]* It's too bad -- after you've set it all so beautifully -- and it's getting so late -- some one might be coming any moment. How's cook?

DUNHAM: Cook's in a temper, as always, madam.

MRS. PRINGLE: I'm glad to hear it. She's like an actress -- the better the temper, the better the performance. As long as she serves us a good dinner I don't care how much she swears. The rest of you can just keep out of her way. Where's Gustave?

DUNHAM: I'm sorry to have to say it, madam, but there's such an awful blizzard out he's sweeping off the sidewalk.

MRS. PRINGLE: Oh! Dear me, yes! I should have ordered an awning! But who expected a storm like this.

[She glances out of the window. ELAINE, a young debutante in evening gown comes running in with a bunch of place-cards.]

ELAINE: Here are the place-cards, mother, and the diagram. Shall I put them around?

MRS. PRINGLE: Yes, dear. Elaine, I'm going up to look after your father. He's so helpless about his ties. *[She starts to leave the room.]* Remove one plate, Dunham.

DUNHAM: Remove one plate, madam? Oh! Madam! It is a certainty! You wouldn't sit down with thirteen.

MRS. PRINGLE: *[Drawing back.]* Thirteen! Why, you're right--thirteen! We can never sit down with thirteen. That's all due to Mr. Harper's negligence. Sick friend, nothing! He's just one of those careless men who never answer their invitations in time. His flowers, indeed, to make me forgive him -- now look at the trouble he's put me to -- thirteen! I wonder whom I could get to come in the last minute. Quick -- Elaine -- help me think.

[She rushes to the telephone and looks madly through her list of acquaintances.]

ELAINE: There's always Uncle George.

MRS. PRINGLE: He never opens his head!

DUNHAM: Mr. Morgan, madam, he always tells a joke or two.

MRS. PRINGLE: Why, yes, Dunham -- that's clever of you! Hello Central -- Lakeview 5971 -- at once, please -- Elaine dear, your hair's much too tight -- pull it out -- pull it out -- come here. *[In telephone.]* Mr. Morgan's Well, this is Mrs. Pringle speaking -- from across the street. Yes. When Mr. Morgan comes in, please tell him to call me up right away. I want him to dine with us -- in about ten minutes -- you expect him? *[She pull's ELAIN'S hair out to make it look fluffier. ELAINE makes faces of pain, but her mother pays no attention.]* Have him call me right away. *[She hangs up the receiver.]* Now if he shouldn't get it -- *then* what'll I do?

ELAINE: Well, mother, *I* don't have to be at the table. It's your party, anyway. Everybody's married and older than I am.

MRS. PRINGLE: *[Pointing to the table diagram in ELAIN'S hand.]* Didn't I put you next to Oliver Farnsworth? Millions! He's worth millions!

ELAINE: Well, he won't be giving me any.

MRS. PRINGLE: Can't he marry you? Aren't you going to try to make a good match for yourself? I fling every eligible man I can at your head. Can't you finish the rest yourself?

ELAINE: It's no use, mother, your trying to marry me off to anyone as important as he is. He frightens me to death. I lose my tongue. I'm as afraid of him as I'd be afraid of the Prince of Wales!

MRS. PRINGLE: The Prince of Wales! Oh! What wouldn't I give to have the Prince of Wales in my house! New York has lost its heart to him. I was just telling Mr. Farnsworth yesterday that I'd give anything to have the Prince here. It would establish my social position for life! And I've such a reputation for being a wonderful hostess. *[The telephone rings.]* Dear me! -- the phone -- Hello -- Mrs. Sedgwick -- Yes -- this is Mrs. Pringle -- What? No -- Oh! Caught in a snow drift -- can't get another car? *[She puts her hand over the telephone and speaks delightedly to ELAINE.]* Good! The widow can't come -- that leaves us twelve -- remove two plates, Dunham. *[DUNHAM removes two plates. and ELAINE changes the table-cards. MRS. PRINGLE continues into the telephone.]* Oh! That's a shame! I'm heartbroken. Oh! My dear, how can we get along without you! But have you really *tried?* Oh, I'm reduced to tears. Good-bye, dear. *[She hangs up the receiver, and takes it down again.]* Well, I'm glad she dropped out -- Central -- give me Lakeview 5971 -- Dunham, with two *less*, you can *save* two cocktails and at least four glasses of champagne. *[Into the telephone.]* Has Mr. Morgan come in yet? Well, don't give him the message I telephoned before about crossing the street to Mrs. Pringle's for dinner. It's too late -- you understand? *[She hangs up the receiver.]* Well, anyway, I've invited Clem, returned my indebtedness and saved my champagne besides--

DUNHAM: The liquor is getting low, madam -- what with prohibition and entertaining so much--

ELAINE: *[In dismay.]* But, mother, if you only have twelve people, Father can't sit at the head of the table.

MRS. PRINGLE: But he *has* to sit at the head. It looks too undignified when the man of the house is pushed to the side--

ELAINE: There's no other way. There must be a woman at each end--

MRS. PRINGLE: *[Distraught.]* How absurd! I always forget. Of course twelve is an impossible number -- *[She goes around the table looking at the place cards.]* I don't want to put any of these women at the head -- there's Mrs. Darby -- such a cat -- I wouldn't give her the honor and Mrs. -- *[The telephone rings.]* Answer it, Dunham.

DUNHAM: Hello -- Mrs. Pringle's residence -- a message? Yes, sir -- What, sir? -- Mr. Darby -- the doctor says your baby has the chicken-pox--

MRS. PRINGLE: Chicken-pox! Elaine!

ELAINE: Mother!

DUNHAM: Yes, sir. *[He hangs up the receiver.]* Mr. Darby sends his apologies -- but owing to the transmutability of the disease, Mr. and Mrs. Darby feel obliged to regret and also their house-guests, Mr. and Mrs. Fleetwood--

MRS. PRINGLE: That's four out.

ELAINE: Then you're only eight! Quick, the plates, Dunham--

[She begins to remove chairs and gathers up silver and plates feverishly. MRS. PRINGLE getting more and more distraught, helps. With so much unaccustomed help, DUNHAM gets confused and goes through many unnecessary motions; removes plates, breaks them, drops silver, aimlessly trying to hurry, his fingers all thumbs.]

MRS. PRINGLE: Don't we know someone to invite the last minute--

ELAINE: The Hatwoods--

MRS. PRINGLE: They don't serve drinks when they entertain -- I can't afford to invite them to drink mine--

ELAINE: The Greens--

MRS. PRINGLE: She's not interesting enough.

ELAINE: Mr. Conley--

MRS. PRINGLE: He never makes a dinner call, even after all the times I have invited him.

ELAINE: Hester Longley--

MRS. PRINGLE: *Not* at the same table with *you* and Oliver Farnsworth. She's far too pretty, too clever--

ELAINE: Where's our book? *[She runs her finger down the address book.]* The Tuppers?

MRS. PRINGLE: The Tuppers! Good Heavens, Elaine, six in the family.

ELAINE: That would get us back to fourteen; then father could sit at the *head* of the table.

MRS. PRINGLE: Well, try them. I'll rush and tell your father to hold up the drawing room-- *[Exit left.]*

ELAINE: *[At the telephone.]* Ridgeway 9325 -- This is Elaine Pringle -- What Tupper am I speaking to? Oh, Ella, hello! -- I hope you haven't finished your dinner -- We had a party arranged here and the last moment everybody's been dropping out -- the blizzard -- Can't you flock your family around the corner and eat with us? Mother and I thought we knew you well enough to call you like this at the seventh hour. You would? Oh! fine! *[To DUNHAM.]* Six more plates, Dunham. *[In the telephone.]* What? -- Oh -- well -- but -- *[She hesitates, stutters, looks distressed, muffles the telephone.]* Dunham, get *Mother* quick. *[In the telephone as DUNHAM hurries out of the room.]* Yes -- yes -- of course *[not enthusiastically]*, love it -- why certainly -- yes, my dear -- all right. *[She hangs up the receiver and puts her hand to her head with an ejaculation of dismay.]* Great Caesar, *now* what have I done?

MRS. PRINGLE: *[Rushes in followed by DUNHAM.]* What's the matter -- Elaine -- what is--

ELAINE: Now I've done it! I've just done it -- but I couldn't get out of it -- I just couldn't -- you weren't here -- I always lose my head and bungle things--

MRS. PRINGLE: But what -- don't keep us waiting like this -- what *is* it?

ELAINE: I invited Ella and the family and she accepted and then she said they had two house-guests -- and would it be all right and of course I said it would and now we're -- *sixteen!*

DUNHAM: *[In dismay.]* Sixteen! But, madam, the table's not that long!

MRS. PRINGLE: Elaine! That's just like you -- no tact -- no worldly wisdom -- if I'd been at the phone I'd have politely said that my table--

ELAINE: But you weren't at the phone -- you ought to attend to such messages yourself -- you know I *always* lose my head --

DUNHAM: But the dishes, madam -- and we only have *fourteen* squabs--

ELAINE: I won't eat any--

MRS. PRINGLE: But I must not be disgraced -- we'll have to make the best of it -- and insert another board -- *[DUNHAM goes out. MRS. PRINGLE and ELAINE hurriedly remove part of the cloth.]*

ELAINE: But mother, I needn't sit at the table.

MRS. PRINGLE: *[Pointing to the chair authoritatively.]* You're *going to sit right next to Oliver Farnsworth!* Now I don't wish to hear another word about it.

ELAINE: But can't we squeeze them in without all the work of adding another board? If I move the plates and chairs closer--

MRS. PRINGLE: Have you forgotten that Mr. Tupper weighs something like two hundred and fifty pounds? And Mrs. Conley has no waist line? It can't be done!--

DUNHAM: *[Entering with table board.]* Cook is in a rage, madam -- she says she has only prepared for fourteen.

MRS. PRINGLE: I can't help it -- she'll have to prepare for *sixteen*. Tell her to open cans of soup and vegetables and--

DUNHAM: But the ice-cream forms and the gelatin molds--

ELAINE: I'll pretend I don't like them.

MRS. PRINGLE: And I'll pretend I'm on a diet--

ELAINE: But I really wouldn't have to be at the *table*.

MRS. PRINGLE: Be still! *[She starts as the telephone rings.]* The telephone! *[Her hand to her head.]* Now what? Don't answer it! It's driving me mad-- *[She goes herself as ELAINE and DUNHAM do not go.]* Hello -- yes -- This is Mrs. Pringle -- Oh! yes -- Jessica! -- what! -- the blizzard -- your cold -- too dangerous! *[She waves to DUNHAM not to put the board in the table. DUNHAM, ELAINE and MRS. PRINGLE are delighted and relieved but MRS. PRINGLE pretends otherwise over the telephone.]* Oh! Jessica -- you poor dear --yes, your husband's right, it would be foolhardy -- put on a mustard plaster -- hot toddy -- go to bed -- so sorry! *[She hangs up the receiver.]* There -- that's *wonderful* -- now we are *just* fourteen--

ELAINE: But the cards are all wrong. Only six are coming who were invited originally. You'll have to make another diagram. How do you want them seated?

MRS. PRINGLE: Give it to me. *[She remains at the telephone table where there is a pad and a pencil and makes a new diagram.]*

ELAINE: Here are some fresh cards. *[She tears up the old cards, then goes back to help DUNHAM, who is having a maddening time with the table.]*

MRS. PRINGLE: What a mess! I spent *hours* over that diagram! So much depends upon having guests seated harmoniously! There's the front door-bell, Dunham -- I told Annie to answer it for you -- but go, peek into the drawing-room and tell me who it is-- *[As DUNHAM goes out, the telephone rings. MRS. PRINGLE eyes it suspiciously.]* You murderous instrument! What have you to say? Now what? *Hello!* Who! Mr. Farnsworth! Mr. *Oliver Farnsworth?* No--you're his *secretary?* He's *what? Instructed* you to make his excuses! He had to leave for Boston at once on very important business -- Oh! *[She hangs up the receiver without completing the conversation and hits the telephone in a temper, then rises and paces back and forth in a rage.]* How *dare* he! How *dare* he! The last moment like this! No regard for a hostess's feelings! No regard for the efforts she goes to to provide an evening's enjoyment! And such a good dinner I planned -- and he promised he would come -- business! I don't believe it! He didn't want to exert himself -- was afraid of freezing in the blizzard -- as if he didn't have half a dozen limousines to carry him to the door -- selfishness -- downright rudeness -- and worth millions -- just a match for you, Elaine -- and I was bound you should meet him and sit next to him at the table *[she tears up his card]*, and now I don't know when I can give you a chance like that again! I'm perfectly furious -- I'll never speak to him again! I won't be treated that way--

ELAINE: *[Timidly.]* Perhaps he really did have business and was called away--

MRS. PRINGLE: *[Not hearing her.]* And I one of the most important hostesses in this city -- people clamoring to receive my invitations -- all my affairs are a success. I insist that they shall be -- I can't bear a failure -- I won't have a failure -- he was my most important guest -- he's such a man's man -- so important financially -- every other man considers it an honor to meet him -- and now not coming! I'm furious! Furious! It's all this damnable blizzard!

ELAINE: Now I *will* have to stay away from the table. His not coming makes us thirteen again.

MRS. PRINGLE: *[In a temper.]* Go to bed -- go up to the nursery! I'll send you milk and crackers!

ELAINE: But, mother, it's not *my* fault that he had business out of town.

MRS. PRINGLE: Yes, it is! If you'd perk up a bit and not be so timid and make something of yourself, he would hear about your attractions from other men and be curious to meet you himself -- Oh! What a family I have! No one to help me with my ambitions! Go to bed! I certainly won't sit down to thirteen -- go to bed -- get out of my sight--

[DUNHAM enters from left.]

DUNHAM: It was Mr. Morgan, madam--

MRS. PRINGLE: Mr. Morgan! But I telephoned his maid to tell him *not* to come.

DUNHAM: He couldn't have received the second message, madam, for I heard him explaining to Mr. Pringle how happy he was to receive your telephone invitation.

ELAINE: That makes you thirteen again -- unless you don't want me to go to bed--

MRS. PRINGLE: Of course I don't want you to go to bed. We're back to where we started -- fourteen, Dunham.

DUNHAM: I'll get the cocktails ready, madam. Annie told me there were several motors making their way through the snow. It's late now and cook's swearing about the dinner getting too dry-- *[The telephone rings. ELAINE jumps.]*

ELAINE: I won't answer it.

MRS. PRINGLE: I should say not -- hello -- what is it? *[Sharply.]* Yes -- yes? Mrs. Tupper! Yes! Mrs. Tupper! But now you *must* come -- we're prepared for you -- yes -- for eight of you -- Your daughter told my daughter about your house-guests and we are delighted to have them -- but now we're *set* for you -- but every plate is set -- but your daughter was quite right -- it wasn't an imposition at all -- but you *must* come now -- of course my daughter had authority to invite the guests of -- Oh -- eight isn't at all a big number -- there is room -- the table is all set -- but I beg of you -- but my dear, you are *not* imposing -- Oh! but how foolish of you to take that stand! Why my dear, my dear -- *[She hangs up the receiver.]* Now, what do you think of that? Mrs. Tupper is perfectly furious at Ella for telling you about the house-guests, and says Ella has no tact; that nothing would induce her to bring eight when we invited six -- so she's leaving Ella and Henry at home -- only six are coming. Remove two plates, Dunham -- we're twelve after all--

ELAINE: But if you leave it twelve, father *can't* sit at the *end*--

MRS. PRINGLE: *[Exhausted, harassed, angry, tempestuous.]* I shall go mad! I'll never entertain again--never--never--people ought to know whether they're coming or not--but they accept and regret and regret and accept--they drive me wild. *[DUNHAM goes out.]* This is my last dinner party--*my very last*--a fiasco--an utter fiasco! A haphazard crowd--hurried together--when I had planned everything so beautifully--now how shall I seat them--how shall I seat them? If I put Mr. Tupper here and Mrs. Conley there then Mrs. Tupper has to sit next to her husband and if I want Mr. Morgan there--Oh! It's impossible--I might as well put their names in a hat and draw them out at random--never again! I'm through! Through with society--with parties--with friends--I wipe my slate clean--they'll miss my entertainments--they'll wish they had been more considerate--after this, I'm going to live for myself! I'm going to be selfish and hard--and unsociable--and drink my liquor myself instead of offering it gratis to the whole town!--I'm *through! Through* with men like Oliver Farnsworth!--I don't care how rich they are! How influential they are--how important they are! They're nothing without courtesy and consideration--business--off on train--nonsense--didn't want to come--didn't want to meet a sweet, pretty girl--didn't want to marry her--well, he's not good enough for you!--don't you marry him! Don't you dare marry him! I won't let you marry him! Do you hear? If you tried to elope or anything like that, I'd break it off--yes, I would--*Oliver Farnsworth* will never get recognition from me!--He is beneath my notice! I hate Oliver Farnsworth!

[DUNHAM enters with a note on a silver plate.]

DUNHAM: A note from Mr. Farnsworth, madam--

MRS. PRINGLE: A note from Mr. Farnsworth! *[She takes and opens it.]*

DUNHAM: Yes, madam, there are two strange gentlemen in the lower hall. They presented this letter. He said he was the secretary. All the other guests are upstairs in the drawing-room, madam, I counted twelve in all, including you and Mr. Pringle and Miss Elaine. But the two gentlemen downstairs, madam, are waiting for your answer -- the one gentlemen's face looked very familiar, madam, but I just can't place him -- although I'm sure I've seen his face somewhere--

MRS. PRINGLE: *[She has been reading the note and is almost fainting with surprise and joy.]* Seen his face -- *somewhere* -- Oh, my goodness! Elaine -- It's the Prince of Wales!

DUNHAM: The secretary said you cut off the telephone or central disconnected you. He was about to tell you that Mr. Farnsworth knew that the blizzard had prevented His Highness from keeping an engagement way up town--

MRS. PRINGLE: The Prince of Wales sitting in my lower hall -- waiting for *me* to ask him to dinner--

ELAINE: Then we'll be thirteen again--

DUNHAM: There's the secretary, Miss, he is his bodyguard--

MRS. PRINGLE: *[Rising to the occasion.]* Certainly, the secretary, Elaine. We shall be fourteen at dinner -- Serve the cocktails, Dunham -- the guests may sit anywhere they choose. I shall bring the Prince in with *me!*

ELAINE: *[Following.]* But mother, wasn't it nice of Oliver Farnsworth to send a Prince in his place?

MRS. PRINGLE: Didn't I always say that Oliver Farnsworth was the most considerate of men?

ELAINE: I think I shall *like* Mr. Farnsworth.

MRS. PRINGLE: Silly child! It is too late now to like Mr. Farnsworth. It's time now to like the Prince. *[Starting out.]* I always manage somehow to be the most successful of hostesses! Thank God for the blizzard!

CURTAIN

THE GENIUS

Horace Holley

CHARACTERS:

THE BOY
THE MAN

[The front porch of a small farmhouse in New England. Stone flags lead to the road; the yard is a careless, comfortable lawn with two or three old maples. It is autumn.]

[A BOY of sixteen or so, carrying a paper parcel, stops hesitatingly, looks in a moment and then walks to the porch. As he stands there a MAN comes out of the house. The man is in his early forties, he stoops a little, but not from weakness; his expression is one of deep calm.]

THE MAN: I wonder if you have seen my dog? I was going for a walk, but Rex seems to have grown tired of waiting.

THE BOY: Your dog? No, sir, I haven't seen him. Shall I go look?

THE MAN: No, never mind. He'll come back. Rex and I understand each other. He has his little moods, like me.

THE BOY: If you were going for a walk—?

THE MAN: It doesn't matter at all. I can go any time. You don't live in this country?

THE BOY: No, sir. I live in New York. I wish I did. It's beautiful here, isn't it?

THE MAN: It's very beautiful to me. I love it. You may have come a long road this morning, let's sit down.

THE BOY: Thank you. I'm not interfering with anything?

THE MAN: Bless your heart! No indeed. What is there to interfere with? All we have is life, and this is part of it.

THE BOY: I like to sit under these trees. It makes me think of the Old Testament.

THE MAN: That's interesting. How?

THE BOY: Well, maybe I'm wrong, but whenever I think of the Old Testament I see an old man under a tree—

THE MAN: Yes?

THE BOY: A man who has lived it all through, you know, and found out something real about it; and he sits there calm and strong, something like a tree himself; and every once in a while somebody comes along—a boy, you know,—and the boy talks to him all about himself, just as we imagine we'd like to with our fathers, if they weren't so busy, or our teachers, if they didn't depend so much upon books, or our ministers, if we thought they would really understand,—and the old man doesn't say much maybe, but the boy goes away much stronger and happier....

THE MAN: Yes, yes, I understand. The Old Testament.... They did get hold of things, didn't they?

THE BOY: What I can't understand is how nowadays people seem more grown up and competent than those men were, in a way, and we do such wonderful things—skyscrapers and aeroplanes—and yet we aren't half so wonderful as they were in the Old Testament with their jugs and their wooden plows. I mean, we aren't near so big as the things we do, while those old fellows were so much bigger. We smile at them, but if some day one of our machines fell over on us what would we do about it?

THE MAN: I wonder.

THE BOY: I went through a big factory just last week. One of my friends' father is the manager, and all I could think of was what could a fellow do who didn't like it, who didn't fit in.... Nowadays most everybody seems competent about factories or business or something like that—you know—and they've got hold of everything, so a fellow's got to do the same thing or where is he?

THE MAN: That's the first question, certainly: where is he? But where is he if he does do the same thing?

THE BOY: Why, he's with the rest. And they don't ask that question....

THE MAN: I'm afraid they don't. It would be interesting to be there if they should begin to ask it, wouldn't it?

THE BOY: Yes.... I'd like to be there when some I know ask themselves! But they never will. Why should they?

THE MAN: Don't you mean how can they?

THE BOY: Yes, of course. They don't ask the question because the big thing they are doing seems to be the answer beforehand. But it isn't! Not compared with the Old Testament. So we have to ask it for ourselves. And that's why I came here....

THE MAN: Oh. You want to know where they are, with their power, or where you will be without it?

THE BOY: Where I'll be. I hate it! But what else is there today?

THE MAN: Why, there's you.

THE BOY: But that's just it! What am I for if I can't join in? I came to you.... You don't mind my talking, do you?

THE MAN: On the contrary.

THE BOY: Well, everybody I know is a part of it, so how could they tell me what to do outside of it? I've been wondering about that for a year. Before then, when I was just a boy, the world seemed full of everything, but now it seems to have only one thing. That or nothing. Then one day I saw a photograph somebody had cut out of a Sunday paper, and I thought to myself there's a man who seems outside, entirely outside, and yet he has something. It wasn't all or nothing for him ... and I wondered who it was. Then I found your book, with the same picture in it. You bet I read it right off! It was the first time in my life I had ever felt power as great as skyscrapers and railroads and yet apart from them. Outside of all they mean. Like the Old Testament. Those poems!

THE MAN: You liked them?

THE BOY: It was more than that. How can a fellow like the ocean, or a snow storm?

THE MAN: Is that what you thought they were like?

THE BOY: Why, they went off like a fourteen inch gun! Not a whine about life in them—not a single regret for anything. They were wonderful! They seemed to pick up mountains and cities and toss them all about like toys. They made me feel that what I was looking for was able to conquer what I didn't like.... I said to myself I don't care if he does laugh at me, I'll go and ask him where all that power is! And so I came....

THE MAN: There's Rex now—over across the road. He's wondering who you are. He sees we are friends, and he's pretending to be jealous. Dogs are funny, aren't they? But you were speaking about my poems. It's odd that their first criticism should come from you like this. You must be about the same age I was when I began writing—when I wanted above anything to write a book like that, and when such a book seemed the most impossible thing I could do. Like trying to swim the Atlantic, or live forever.

THE BOY: It seemed impossible? I should think it would be the most natural thing in the world, for you—like eating dinner.

THE MAN: That's the wonderful thing—not the book, but that I should have come to write it!

THE BOY: But who else could write it?

THE MAN: At your age I thought anybody could—anybody and everybody except myself.

THE BOY: Really?

THE MAN: Really and truly. You've no idea what a useless misfit I was.

THE BOY: But I read somewhere you had always been brilliant, even as a boy.

THE MAN: Unfortunately ... yes. That was what made it so hard for me. Shall I tell you about it?

THE BOY: I wish you would!

THE MAN: Brilliance—I'll tell you what that was, at least for me. I wrote several things that people called "brilliant." One in particular, a little play of decadent epigram. It was acted by amateurs before an admiring "select" audience. That was when I was twenty-one. From about sixteen on I had been acutely miserable—physically miserable. I never knew when I wouldn't actually cave in. I felt like a bankrupt living on borrowed money. Of course, it's plain enough now—the revolt of starved nerves. I cared only for my mind, grew only in that, and the rest of me withered up like a stalk in dry soil. So the flower drooped too—in decadent epigram. But nobody pointed out the truth of it all to me, and I scorned to give my body a thought. People predicted a brilliant future—for me, crying inside! Then I married. I married the girl who had taken the star part in the play. According to the logic of the situation, it was inevitable. Everybody remarked how inevitable it was. A decorative girl, you know. She wanted to be the wife of a great man.... Well, we didn't get along. There was an honest streak in me somewhere which hated deception. I couldn't play the part of "brilliant" young poet with any success. She was at me all the while to write more of the same thing. And I didn't want to. The difference between the "great" man I was supposed to be and the sick child I really was, began to torture. I knew I oughtn't to go on any further if I wanted to do anything real. Then one night we had an "artistic" dinner. My wife had gotten hold of a famous English poet, and through him a publisher. The publisher was her real game. I drank champagne before dinner so as to be "brilliant." I was. And before I realized it, Norah had secured a promise from the publisher to bring out a book of plays. I remember she said it was practically finished. But it wasn't, only the one, and I hated that. But I sat down conscientiously to write the book that she, and apparently all the world that counted, expected me to write. Well, I couldn't write it. Not a blessed word! Something inside me refused to work. And there I was. In a month or so she began to ask about it. Norah thought I ought to turn them out while she waited. I walked up and down the park one afternoon wondering what to tell her.... And when I realized that either she would never understand or would despise me, I grew desperate. I wrote her a note, full of fine phrases about "incompatibility," her "unapproachable ideals," the "soul's need of freedom"—things she would understand and wear a heroic attitude about—and fled. I came here....

THE BOY: Of course. But didn't she follow you? Didn't they bother you?

THE MAN: Not a bit. Norah preferred her lonely heroism. In a few months I was quite forgotten. That was one of the healthful things I learned. Well, I was a wreck when I came here, I wanted only to lie down under a tree.... And there it was, under that tree yonder, my salvation came.

THE BOY: Your salvation?

THE MAN: Hunger. That was my salvation. Simple, elemental, inescapable appetite. You see I had no servant, no one at all. So I had to get up and work to prepare my food.... It was very strange. Compared with this life, my life before had been like living in a locked box. Some one to do everything for me except think, and consequently I thought too much. But here the very fact of life was brought home to me. I spent weeks working about the house and grounds on the common necessities. By the time winter came on the place was fit to live in—and I was enjoying life. All the "brilliance" had faded away; I was as simple as a blade of grass. For a year I didn't write a word. I had the courage to wait for the real thing, nobody pestering me to be a "genius"! Some day you may read that first book. People said I had re-discovered the virtue of humility. I had.

THE BOY: I will read it! And how much more it will mean to me now!

THE MAN: I suppose you know the theory about vibrations—how if a little push is given a bridge, and repeated often enough at the right intervals, the bridge will fall?

THE BOY: Yes.

THE MAN: Well, that's the whole secret of what you have been looking for—what you found in my poems.

THE BOY: I don't understand.

THE MAN: A man's life is a rhythm. Eating, sleeping, working, playing, loving, thinking—everything. And when we live so that each activity comes at the right interval, we gain power. When one interrupts another, we lose. Weakness is merely the thrust of one impulse against another, instead of their combined thrust against the world. When I came here, feeling like a criminal, I was obeying the one right instinct in a welter of emotions. It was like the faintest of heart beats in a sick body. I listened to that. Then I learned physical hunger, then sleep, and so on. It's incredible how stupid I was about the elemental art of living! I had to begin all over from the beginning, as if no one had ever lived before.

THE BOY: That's what you meant in your poems about religion.

THE MAN: Exactly! I learned that "good" is the rhythm of the man's personal nature, and that "evil" is merely the confusion of the same impulses. As time went on it became instinctive to live for and by the rhythm. Everything about my life here was caught up and used in the vision of power—drawing water, cutting wood, digging in the garden, dawn. It was all marvelous—I couldn't help writing those poems. They are the natural joys and sorrows of ten years. As a matter of fact, though, I grew to care less and less about writing, as living became fuller and richer. People write too much. They would write less if they had to make the fire in the morning.

THE BOY: The first impulse ... I see. Oh, life might be so simple!

THE MAN: Why not? The animals have it. Men have it at times, but we make each other forget. If we could only be each other's reminders instead of forgetters!

THE BOY: Yes! But I see the only thing to do is to go away, like you.

THE MAN: Not necessarily, I was merely a bad case, and required a desperate remedy, earth and air and freedom from others' will. I need the country, but the next man might require the city as passionately. Don't imagine that only the hermits, like me, live instinctively. It can be done in New York, too, only one mustn't be so sensitive to others.... After all, friend, we were wrong in saying that this power lies outside the world of skyscrapers and business. It doesn't lie outside nor inside. It cuts across everything. Do you see? For it's all a matter of the man's own soul.

THE BOY: Then?

THE MAN: We can't live in a vacuum. The more you feel the force, the more you must act. The more you can act. And in the long run it doesn't matter what you do, if you do what your own instinct bids.

THE BOY: Then I could stay right in the midst of it?

THE MAN: Yes. And if you were thinking of writing poetry, it might even be better to stay in the midst of it. Drama, you know ... and it's time for a new drama.

THE BOY: It isn't that, with me. I can't write.... I had one splendid teacher. He used to talk about things right in class. He said that most educated people think that intellect is a matter of making fine distinctions—of seeing as two separate points what the unintelligent would believe was one point; but that this idea was finicky. He wanted us to see that intelligence might also be a matter of seeing the connection between two things so far apart that most people would think they were always separate. I like that. It made education mean something, because it made it depend on imagination instead of grubbing. And then he told us about the history of our subject—grammar. How it began as poetry, when every word was an original creation; and then became philosophy, as people had to arrange speech with thought; and then science, with more or less exact, laws. I could see it—the thing became alive. And he said all knowledge passed through the same stages, and there isn't anything that can't eventually be made scientific. That made me think a good deal. I wondered if somebody couldn't work out a way of preventing anybody from being poor. It seems so unnecessary, with so much work being done. That's what I want to do. Thanks to you, I—

THE MAN: Here's Rex! Rex, know my good friend. I know you will like him. Rex always cares for the people I do, don't you, Rex?

THE BOY: Of course, I see one thing: it's the people nearest one that make the most difference. Mother, now, she will understand.... You don't believe in marrying, though, do you?

THE MAN: I certainly do!

THE BOY: But I thought—

THE MAN: You thought because I left one woman and hadn't found another that I didn't care for women? Others believe that, too, but it isn't so. On the contrary. You see, I didn't so much leave her as get away from my own failure. Of course, there is such a thing as the wrong woman. She makes a man a fraction. The better she is in herself, the less she leaves him to live by. One twentieth is less than one half. But the right woman! She multiplies a man....

THE BOY: Oh!

THE MAN: Why, you might have told from my poems how I believe in love.

THE BOY: I don't remember any love poems.

THE MAN: Bless your heart! Every one of them was a love poem. Not the old-fashioned kind, about fading roses and tender hearts.... I sent that book out as a cry for the mate. It is charged with the fullness of love. That's why I could write about trees and storms.

THE BOY: I suppose if I had been older....

THE MAN: It isn't one's age but one's need. She will understand. Look, the sun has gone round the corner of the house. Is that lunch you have in the parcel?

THE BOY: Yes.

THE MAN: Would you like to make it a picnic? I'll get something from the house, and then we can walk to the woods.

THE BOY: I'd love to!

THE MAN: All right, I'll be ready in no time. Come, Rex!

CURTAIN

RIDERS TO THE SEA

John Millington Synge

CHARACTERS:

MAURYA, an old woman
BARTLEY, her son
CATHLEEN, her daughter
NORA, a younger daughter
MEN AND WOMEN

[An island off the West of Ireland. Cottage kitchen, with nets, oilskins, spinning-wheel, some new boards standing by the wall, etc. CATHLEEN, a girl of about twenty, finishes kneading cake, and puts it down in the pot-oven by the fire; then wipes her hands, and begins to spin at the wheel. NORA, a young girl, puts her head in at the door.]

NORA: *(in a low voice)* Where is she?

CATHLEEN: She's lying down, God help her, and maybe sleeping, if she's able.

[NORA comes in softly, and takes a bundle from under her shawl.]

CATHLEEN: *(spinning the wheel rapidly)* What is it you have?

NORA: The young priest is after bringing them. It's a shirt and a plain stocking were got off a drowned man in Donegal.

[CATHLEEN stops her wheel with a sudden movement, and leans out to listen.]

NORA: We're to find out if it's Michael's they are; some time herself will be down looking by the sea.

CATHLEEN: How would they be Michael's, Nora? How would he go the length of that way to the far north?

NORA: The young priest says he's known the like of it. "If it's Michael's they are," says he, "you can tell herself he's got a clean burial by the grace of God, and if they're not his, let no one say a word about them, for she'll be getting her death," says he, "with crying and lamenting."

[The door which NORA half closed is blown open by a gust of wind.]

CATHLEEN: *(looking out anxiously)* Did you ask him would he stop Bartley going this day with the horses to the Galway fair?

NORA: "I won't stop him," says he, "but let you not be afraid. Herself does be saying prayers half through the night, and the Almighty God won't leave her destitute," says he, "with no son living."

CATHLEEN: Is the sea bad by the white rocks, Nora?

NORA: Middling bad, God help us. There's a great roaring in the west, and it's worse it'll be getting when the tide's turned to the wind. *[She goes over to the table with the bundle.]* Shall I open it now?

CATHLEEN: Maybe she'd wake up on us, and come in before we'd done. *[Coming to the table]* It's a long time we'll be, and the two of us crying.

NORA: *(goes to the inner door and listens)* She's moving about on the bed. She'll be coming in a minute.

CATHLEEN: Give me the ladder, and I'll put them up in the turf-loft, the way she won't know of them at all, and maybe when the tide turns she'll be going down to see would he be floating from the east.

[They put the ladder against the gable of the chimney; CATHLEEN goes up a few steps and hides the bundle in the turf-loft. MAURYA comes from the inner room.]

MAURYA: *(looking up at CATHLEEN and speaking querulously)* Isn't it turf enough you have for this day and evening?

CATHLEEN: There's a cake baking at the fire for a short space *(throwing down the turf)* and Bartley will want it when the tide turns if he goes to Connemara.

[NORA picks up the turf and puts it round the pot-oven.]

MAURYA: *(sitting down on a stool at the fire)* He won't go this day with the wind rising from the south and west. He won't go this day, for the young priest will stop him surely.

NORA: He'll not stop him, mother, and I heard Eamon Simon and Stephen Pheety and Colum Shawn saying he would go.

MAURYA: Where is he itself?

NORA: He went down to see would there be another boat sailing in the week, and I'm thinking it won't be long till he's here now, for the tide's turning at the green head, and the hooker's tacking from the east.

CATHLEEN: I hear someone passing the big stones.

NORA: *(looking out)* He's coming now, and he in a hurry.

BARTLEY: *(comes in and looks round the room; speaking sadly and quietly)* Where is the bit of new rope, Cathleen, was bought in Connemara?

CATHLEEN: *(coming down)* Give it to him, Nora; it's on a nail by the white boards. I hung it up this morning, for the pig with the black feet was eating it.

NORA: *(giving him a rope)* Is that it, Bartley?

MAURYA: You'd do right to leave that rope, Bartley, hanging by the boards. *(BARTLEY takes the rope.)* It will be wanting in this place, I'm telling you, if Michael is washed up to-morrow morning, or the next morning, or any morning in the week, for it's a deep grave we'll make him by the grace of God.

BARTLEY: *(beginning to work with the rope)* I've no halter the way I can ride down on the mare, and I must go now quickly. This is the one boat going for two weeks or beyond it, and the fair will be a good fair for horses, I heard them saying below.

MAURYA: It's a hard thing they'll be saying below if the body is washed up and there's no man in it to make the coffin, and I after giving a big price for the finest white boards you'd find in Connemara.

[She looks round at the boards.]

BARTLEY: How would it be washed up, and we after looking each day for nine days, and a strong wind blowing a while back from the west and south?

MAURYA: If it wasn't found itself, that wind is raising the sea, and there was a star up against the moon, and it rising in the night. If it was a hundred horses, or a thousand horses you had itself, what is the price of a thousand horses against a son where there is one son only?

BARTLEY: *(working at the halter, to CATHLEEN)* Let you go down each day, and see the sheep aren't jumping in on the rye, and if the jobber comes you can sell the pig with the black feet if there is a good price going.

MAURYA: How would the like of her get a good price for a pig?

BARTLEY: *(to CATHLEEN)* If the west wind holds with the last bit of the moon let you and Nora get up weed enough for another cock for the kelp. It's hard set we'll be from this day with no one in it but one man to work.

MAURYA: It's hard set we'll be surely the day you're drown'd with the rest. What way will I live and the girls with me, and I an old woman looking for the grave?

[BARTLEY lays down the halter, takes off his old coat, and puts on a newer one of the same flannel.]

BARTLEY: *(to NORA)* Is she coming to the pier?

NORA: *(looking out)* She's passing the green head and letting fall her sails.

BARTLEY: *(getting his purse and tobacco)* I'll have half an hour to go down, and you'll see me coming again in two days, or in three days, or maybe in four days if the wind is bad.

MAURYA: *(turning round to the fire, and putting her shawl over her head)* Isn't it a hard and cruel man won't hear a word from an old woman, and she holding him from the sea?

CATHLEEN: It's the life of a young man to be going on the sea, and who would listen to an old woman with one thing and she saying it over?

BARTLEY: *(taking the halter)* I must go now quickly. I'll ride down on the red mare, and the gray pony'll run behind me. The blessing of God on you.

[He goes out.]

MAURYA: *(crying out as he is in the door)* He's gone now, God spare us, and we'll not see him again. He's gone now, and when the black night is falling I'll have no son left me in the world.

CATHLEEN: Why wouldn't you give him your blessing and he looking round in the door? Isn't it sorrow enough is on everyone in this house without your sending him out with an unlucky word behind him, and a hard word in his ear?

[MAURYA takes up the tongs and begins raking the fire aimlessly without looking round.]

NORA: *(turning towards her)* You're taking away the turf from the cake.

CATHLEEN: *(crying out)* The Son of God forgive us, Nora, we're after forgetting his bit of bread.

[She comes over to the fire.]

NORA: And it's destroyed he'll be going till dark night, and he after eating nothing since the sun went up.

CATHLEEN: *(turning the cake out of the oven)* It's destroyed he'll be, surely. There's no sense left on any person in a house where an old woman will be talking for ever.

[MAURYA sways herself on her stool.]

CATHLEEN: *(cutting off some of the bread and rolling it in a cloth, to MAURYA)* Let you go down now to the spring well and give him this and he passing. You'll see him then and the dark word will be broken, and you can say, "God speed you," the way he'll be easy in his mind.

MAURYA: *(taking the bread)* Will I be in it as soon as himself?

CATHLEEN: If you go now quickly.

MAURYA: *(standing up unsteadily)* It's hard set I am to walk.

CATHLEEN: *(looking at her anxiously)* Give her the stick, Nora, or maybe she'll slip on the big stones.

NORA: What stick?

CATHLEEN: The stick Michael brought from Connemara.

MAURYA: *(taking a stick NORA gives her)* In the big world the old people do be leaving things after them for their sons and children, but in this place it is the young men do be leaving things behind for them that do be old.

[She goes out slowly. NORA goes over to the ladder.]

CATHLEEN: Wait, Nora, maybe she'd turn back quickly. She's that sorry, God help her, you wouldn't know the thing she'd do.

NORA: Is she gone round by the bush?

CATHLEEN: *(looking out)* She's gone now. Throw it down quickly, for the Lord knows when she'll be out of it again.

NORA: *(getting the bundle from the loft)* The young priest said he'd be passing tomorrow, and we might go down and speak to him below if it's Michael's they are surely.

CATHLEEN: *(taking the bundle)* Did he say what way they were found?

NORA: *(coming down)* "There were two men," says he, "and they rowing round with poteen before the cocks crowed, and the oar of one of them caught the body, and they passing the black cliffs of the north."

CATHLEEN: *(trying to open the bundle)* Give me a knife, Nora; the string's perished with the salt water, and there's a black knot on it you wouldn't loosen in a week.

NORA: *(giving her a knife)* I've heard tell it was a long way to Donegal.

CATHLEEN: *(cutting the string)* It is surely. There was a man in here a while ago--the man sold us that knife--and he said if you set off walking from the rocks beyond, it would be seven days you'd be in Donegal.

NORA: And what time would a man take, and he floating?

[CATHLEEN opens the bundle and takes out a bit of a stocking. They look at them eagerly.]

CATHLEEN: *(in a low voice)* The Lord spare us, Nora! Isn't it a queer hard thing to say if it's his they are surely?

NORA: I'll get his shirt off the hook the way we can put the one flannel on the other. *(She looks through some clothes hanging in the corner.)* It's not with them, Cathleen, and where will it be?

CATHLEEN: I'm thinking Bartley put it on him in the morning, for his own shirt was heavy with the salt in it. *(Pointing to the corner)* There's a bit of a sleeve was of the same stuff. Give me that and it will do.

[NORA brings it to her and they compare the flannel.]

CATHLEEN: It's the same stuff, Nora; but if it is itself, aren't there great rolls of it in the shops of Galway, and isn't it many another man may have a shirt of it as well as Michael himself?

NORA: *(who has taken up the stocking and counted the stitches, crying out)* It's Michael, Cathleen, it's Michael; God spare his soul and what will herself say when she hears this story, and Bartley on the sea?

CATHLEEN: *(taking the stocking)* It's a plain stocking.

NORA: It's the second one of the third pair I knitted, and I put up three score stitches, and I dropped four of them.

CATHLEEN: *(counts the stitches)* It's that number is in it. *(Crying out)* Ah, Nora, isn't it a bitter thing to think of him floating that way to the far north, and no one to keen him but the black hags that do be flying on the sea?

NORA: *(swinging herself round, and throwing out her arms on the clothes)* And isn't it a pitiful thing when there is nothing left of a man who was a great rower and fisher, but a bit of an old shirt and a plain stocking?

CATHLEEN: *(after an instant)* Tell me is herself coming, Nora? I hear a little sound on the path.

NORA: *(looking out)* She is, Cathleen. She's coming up to the door.

CATHLEEN: Put these things away before she'll come in. Maybe it's easier she'll be after giving her blessing to Bartley, and we won't let on we've heard anything the time he's on the sea.

NORA: *(helping CATHLEEN to close the bundle)* We'll put them here in the corner.

[They put them into a hole in the chimney corner. CATHLEEN goes back to the spinning wheel.]

NORA: Will she see it was crying I was?

CATHLEEN: Keep your back to the door the way the light'll not be on you.

[NORA sits down at the chimney corner, with her back to the door. MAURYA comes in very slowly, without looking at the girls, and goes over to her stool at the other side of the fire. The cloth with the bread is still in her hand. The girls look at each other, and NORA points to the bundle of bread.]

CATHLEEN: *(after spinning for a moment)* You didn't give him his bit of bread?

[MAURYA begins to keen softly, without turning round.]

CATHLEEN: Did you see him riding down?

[MAURYA goes on keening.]

CATHLEEN: *(a little impatiently)* God forgive you; isn't it a better thing to raise your voice and tell what you seen, than to be making lamentation for a thing that's done? Did you see Bartley, I'm saying to you.

MAURYA: *(with a weak voice)* My heart's broken from this day.

CATHLEEN: *(as before)* Did you see Bartley?

MAURYA: I seen the fearfulest thing.

CATHLEEN: *(leaves her wheel and looks out)* God forgive you; he's riding the mare now over the green head, and the gray pony behind him.

MAURYA: *(starts, so that her shawl falls back from her head and shows her white tossed hair; with a frightened voice)* The gray pony behind him.

CATHLEEN: *(coming to the fire)* What is it ails you, at all?

MAURYA: *(speaking very slowly)* I've seen the fearfulest thing any person has seen, since the day Bride Dara seen the dead man with the child in his arms.

CATHLEEN AND NORA: Uah.

[They crouch down in front of the old woman at the fire.]

NORA: Tell us what it is you seen.

MAURYA: I went down to the spring-well, and I stood there saying a prayer to myself. Then Bartley came along, and he riding on the red mare with the gray pony behind him. *(She puts up her hands, as if to hide something from her eyes.)* The Son of God spare us, Nora!

CATHLEEN: What is it you seen?

MAURYA: I seen Michael himself.   .

CATHLEEN: *(speaking softly)* You did not, mother; it wasn't Michael you seen, for his body is after being found in the far north, and he's got a clean burial by the grace of God.

MAURYA: *(a little defiantly)* I'm after seeing him this day, and he riding and galloping. Bartley came first on the red mare; and I tried to say "God speed you," but something choked the words in my throat. He went by quickly; and, "The blessing of God on you," says he, and I could say nothing. I looked up then, and I crying, at the gray pony, and there was Michael upon it--with fine clothes on him, and new shoes on his feet.

CATHLEEN: *(begins to keen)* It's destroyed we are from this day. It's destroyed, surely.

NORA: Didn't the young priest say the Almighty God wouldn't leave her destitute with no son living?

MAURYA: *(in a low voice, but clearly)* It's little the like of him knows of the sea.... Bartley will be lost now, and let you call in Eamon and make me a good coffin out of the white boards, for I won't live after them. I've had a husband, and a husband's father, and six sons in this house--six fine men, though it was a hard birth I had with every one of them and they coming to the world--and some of them were found and some of them were not found, but they're gone now, the lot of them.... There were Stephen, and Shawn, were lost in the great wind, and found after in the Bay of Gregory of the Golden Mouth, and carried up the two of them on the one plank, and in by that door.

[She pauses for a moment, the girls start as if they heard something through the door that is half-open behind them.]

NORA: *(in a whisper)* Did you hear that, Cathleen? Did you hear a noise in the northeast?

CATHLEEN: *(in a whisper)* There's someone after crying out by the seashore.

MAURYA: *(continues without hearing anything)* There was Sheamus and his father, and his own father again, were lost in a dark night, and not a stick or sign was seen of them when the sun went up. There was Patch after was drowned out of a curagh that turned over. I was sitting here with Bartley, and he a baby, lying on my two knees, and I seen two women, and three women, and four women coming in, and they crossing themselves, and not saying a word. I looked out then, and there were men coming after them, and they holding a thing in the half of a red sail, and water dripping out of it--it was a dry day, Nora--and leaving a track to the door.

[She pauses again with her hand stretched out towards the door. It opens softly and old women begin to come in, crossing themselves on the threshold, and kneeling down in front of the stage with red petticoats over their heads.]

MAURYA: *(half in a dream, to Cathleen)* Is it Patch, or Michael, or what is it at all?

CATHLEEN: Michael is after being found in the far north, and when he is found there how could he be here in this place?

MAURYA: There does be a power of young men floating round in the sea, and what way would they know if it was Michael they had, or another man like him, for when a man is nine days in the sea, and the wind blowing, it's hard set his own mother would be to say what man was it.

CATHLEEN: It's Michael, God spare him, for they're after sending us a bit of his clothes from the far north.

[She reaches out and hands MAURYA the clothes that belonged to MICHAEL. MAURYA stands up slowly, and takes them in her hands. NORA looks out.]

NORA: They're carrying a thing among them and there's water dripping out of it and leaving a track by the big stones.

CATHLEEN: *(in a whisper to the women who have come in)* Is it Bartley it is?

ONE OF THE WOMEN: It is surely, God rest his soul.

[Two younger women come in and pull out the table. Then men carry in the body of BARTLEY, laid on a plank, with a bit of a sail over it, and lay it on the table.]

CATHLEEN: *(to the women, as they are doing so)* What way was he drowned?

ONE OF THE WOMEN: The gray pony knocked him into the sea, and he was washed out where there is a great surf on the white rocks.

[MAURYA has gone over and knelt down at the head of the table. The women are keening softly and swaying themselves with a slow movement. CATHLEEN and NORA kneel at the other end of the table. The men kneel near the door.]

MAURYA: *(raising her head and speaking as if she did not see the people around her)* They're all gone now, and there isn't anything more the sea can do to me.... I'll have no call now to be up crying and praying when the wind breaks from the south, and you can hear the surf is in the east, and the surf is in the west, making a great stir with the two noises, and they hitting one on the other. I'll have no call now to be going down and getting Holy Water in the dark nights after Samhain, and I won't care what way the sea is when the other women will be keening. *(To NORA)* Give me the Holy Water, Nora; there's a small sup still on the dresser.

[NORA gives it to her.]

MAURYA: *(drops MICHAEL'S clothes across BARTLEY'S feet, and sprinkles the Holy Water over him)* It isn't that I haven't prayed for you, Bartley, to the Almighty God. It isn't that I haven't said prayers in the dark night till you wouldn't know what I'd be saying; but it's a great rest I'll have now, and it's time surely. It's a great rest I'll have now, and great sleeping in the long nights after Samhain, if it's only a bit of wet flour we do have to eat, and maybe a fish that would be stinking.

[She kneels down again, crossing herself, and saying prayers under her breath.]

CATHLEEN: *(to an old man)* Maybe yourself and Eamon would make a coffin when the sun rises. We have fine white boards herself bought, God help her, thinking Michael would be found, and I have a new cake you can eat while you'll be working.

THE OLD MAN: *(looking at the boards)* Are there nails with them?

CATHLEEN: There are not, Colum; we didn't think of the nails.

ANOTHER MAN: It's a great wonder she wouldn't think of the nails, and all the coffins she's seen made already.

CATHLEEN: It's getting old she is, and broken.

[MAURYA stands up again very slowly and spreads out the pieces of MICHAEL'S clothes beside the body, sprinkling them with the last of the Holy Water.]

NORA: *(in a whisper to CATHLEEN)* She's quiet now and easy; but the day Michael was drowned you could hear her crying out from this to the spring-well. It's fonder she was of Michael, and would anyone have thought that?

CATHLEEN: *(slowly and clearly)* An old woman will be soon tired with anything she will do, and isn't it nine days herself is after crying and keening, and making great sorrow in the house?

MAURYA: *(puts the empty cup mouth downwards on the table, and lays her hands together on BARTLEY'S feet)* They're all together this time, and the end is come. May the Almighty God have mercy on Bartley's soul, and on Michael's soul, and on the souls of Sheamus and Patch, and Stephen and Shawn *(bending her head);* and may He have mercy on my soul, Nora, and on the soul of everyone is left living in the world.

[She pauses, and the keen rises a little more loudly from the women, then sinks away.]

MAURYA: Michael has a clean burial in the far north, by the grace of the Almighty God. Bartley will have a fine coffin out of the white boards, and a deep grave surely. What more can we want than that? No man at all can be living for ever, and we must be satisfied.

[She kneels down again, and the curtain falls slowly.]

END of PLAY

A MATTER OF HUSBANDS

Ferenc Molnar

Translated by Benjamin Glazer

CHARACTERS:

Famous Actress
Earnest Young Woman

[The scene is a drawing room, but a screen, a sofa and a chair will do, provided that the design and colorings are exotic and suggestive of the apartment of the famous Hungarian actress in which this dialogue takes place. The time is late afternoon, and when the curtain rises the Earnest Young Woman is discovered, poised nervously on the edge of a gilt chair. It is plain she has been sitting there a long time. For perhaps the fiftieth time she is studying the furnishings of the room and regarding the curtained door with a glance that would be impatient if it were not so palpably frightened. And now and then she licks her lips as if her mouth was dry. She is dressed in a very modest frock and wears her hat and furs. At last the Famous Actress enters through the curtained door at the right which leads to her boudoir.]

FAMOUS ACTRESS: You wished to see me?

EARNEST YOUNG WOMAN: *[She gulps emotionally.]* Yes.

FAMOUS ACTRESS: What can I do for you?

EARNEST YOUNG WOMAN: *[Extends her arms in a beseeching gesture.]* Give me back my husband!

FAMOUS ACTRESS: Give you back your husband?!

EARNEST YOUNG WOMAN: Yes. *[The FAMOUS ACTRESS only stares at her in speechless bewilderment.]* You are wondering which one he is.... He is a blond man, not very tall, wears spectacles. He is a lawyer, your manager's lawyer. Alfred is his first name.

FAMOUS ACTRESS: Oh! I have met him--yes.

EARNEST YOUNG WOMAN: I know you have. I implore you, give him back to me.

[There is a long pause.]

FAMOUS ACTRESS: You mustn't mistake my silence for embarrassment. I am at a loss because--I don't quite see how I can give you back your husband when I haven't got him to give.

EARNEST YOUNG WOMAN: You just admitted that you knew him.

FAMOUS ACTRESS: That scarcely implies that I have taken him from you. Of course I know him. He drew up my last contract. And it seems to me I have seen him once or twice since then--backstage. A rather nice-spoken, fair-haired man. Did you say he wore spectacles?

EARNEST YOUNG WOMAN: Yes.

FAMOUS ACTRESS: I don't remember him with spectacles.

EARNEST YOUNG WOMAN: He probably took them off. He wanted to look his best to you. He is in love with you. He never takes them off when I'm around. He doesn't care how he looks when I'm around. He doesn't love me. I implore you, give him back to me!

FAMOUS ACTRESS: If you weren't such a very foolish young woman I should be very angry with you. Wherever did you get the idea that I have taken your husband from you?

EARNEST YOUNG WOMAN: He sends you flowers all the time.

FAMOUS ACTRESS: That's not true.

EARNEST YOUNG WOMAN: It is!

FAMOUS ACTRESS: It isn't. He never sent me a flower in all his life. Did he tell you he did?

EARNEST YOUNG WOMAN: No. I found out at the florist's. The flowers are sent to your dressing room twice a week and charged to him.

FAMOUS ACTRESS: That's a lie.

EARNEST YOUNG WOMAN: Do you mean to say that *I* am lying?

FAMOUS ACTRESS: I mean to say that *someone* is lying to you.

EARNEST YOUNG WOMAN: *[Fumbles in her bag for a letter]* And what about this letter?

FAMOUS ACTRESS: Letter?

EARNEST YOUNG WOMAN: He wrote it to you. And he said--

FAMOUS ACTRESS: He wrote it to me? Let me see.

EARNEST YOUNG WOMAN: No. I'll read it to you. *[She opens it and reads mournfully.]* "My darling, Shan't be able to call for you at the theater tonight. Urgent business. A thousand apologies. Ten thousand kisses. Alfred."

FAMOUS ACTRESS: Oh!

EARNEST YOUNG WOMAN: I found it on his desk this morning. He probably intended to send it to the theater by messenger. But he forgot it. And I opened it. *[She weeps.]*

FAMOUS ACTRESS: You mustn't cry.

EARNEST YOUNG WOMAN: *[Sobbing.]* Why mustn't I? You steal my husband and I mustn't cry! Oh, I know how little it means to you. And how easy it is for you. One night you dress like a royal princess, and the next night you undress like a Greek goddess. You blacken your eyebrows and redden your lips and wax your lashes and paint your face. You have cosmetics and bright lights to make you seem beautiful. An author's lines to make you seem witty and wise. No wonder a poor, simple-minded lawyer falls in love with you. What chance have I against you in my cheap little frock, my own lips and eyebrows, my own unstudied ways? I don't know how to strut and pose and lure a man. I haven't got Mr. Shakespeare to write beautiful speeches for me. In reality you may be more stupid than I am, but I admit that when it comes to alluring men I am no match for you.

FAMOUS ACTRESS: *[Without anger, slowly, regards her appraisingly.]* This is a very interesting case.

EARNEST YOUNG WOMAN: What is?

FAMOUS ACTRESS: Yours.

EARNEST YOUNG WOMAN: Mine? What do you mean?

FAMOUS ACTRESS: I mean that I never received a flower, or a letter, or anything else from your husband. Tell me, haven't you and your husband been getting on rather badly of late?

EARNEST YOUNG WOMAN: Yes, of course.

FAMOUS ACTRESS: You used to be very affectionate to each other?

EARNEST YOUNG WOMAN: Why, yes.

FAMOUS ACTRESS: And of late you have been quite cold?

EARNEST YOUNG WOMAN: Yes.

FAMOUS ACTRESS: Of course! A typical case.... My dear, if you knew how often we actresses meet this sort of thing! It is perfectly clear that your husband has been playing a little comedy to make you jealous, to revive your interest in him.

EARNEST YOUNG WOMAN: *[Dumbfounded, staring.]* Do you really think that? Do you mean to say such a thing has happened to you before?

FAMOUS ACTRESS: Endless times. It happens to every actress who is moderately pretty and successful. It is one of the oldest expedients in the world, and we actresses are such conspicuous targets for it! There is scarcely a man connected with the theater who doesn't make use of us in that way some time or another--authors, composers, scene designers, lawyers, orchestra leaders, even the managers themselves. To regain a wife or sweetheart's affections all they need to do is invent a love affair with one of us. The wife is always so ready to believe it. Usually we don't know a thing about it. But even when it is brought to our notice we don't mind so much. At least we have the consolation of knowing that we are the means of making many a marriage happy which might otherwise have ended in the divorce court.

EARNEST YOUNG WOMAN: But how--how could I know?

FAMOUS ACTRESS: *[With a gracious little laugh.]* There, dear, you mustn't apologize. You couldn't know, of course. It seems so plausible. You fancy your husband in an atmosphere of perpetual temptation, in a backstage world full of beautiful sirens without scruples or morals. One actress, you suppose, is more dangerous than a hundred ordinary women. You hate us and fear us. None understands that better than your husband, who is evidently a very cunning lawyer. And so he plays on your fear and jealousy to regain the love you deny him. He writes a letter and leaves it behind him on the desk. Trust a lawyer never to do that unintentionally. He orders flowers for me by telephone in the morning and probably cancels the order the moment he reaches his office. By the way, hasn't he a lock of my hair?

EARNEST YOUNG WOMAN: Yes. In his desk drawer. I brought it with me.

FAMOUS ACTRESS: Yes. They bribe my hair-dresser to steal from me. It is a wonder I have any hair left at all.

EARNEST YOUNG WOMAN: *[Happily.]* Is that how he got it?

FAMOUS ACTRESS: I can't imagine how else. Tell me, hasn't he left any of my love letters lying around?

EARNEST YOUNG WOMAN: *[In alarm.]* No.

FAMOUS ACTRESS: Don't be alarmed. I haven't written him any.

EARNEST YOUNG WOMAN: Then what made you--?

FAMOUS ACTRESS: I might have if he had come to me frankly and said: "I say, Sara, will you do something for me? My wife and I aren't getting on so well. Would you write me a passionate love letter that I can leave lying around at home where she may find it?" I should certainly have done it for him. I'd have written a letter that would have made you weep into your pillow for a fortnight. I wrote ten like that for a very eminent playwright once. But he had no luck with them. His wife was such a proper person she returned them all to him unread.

EARNEST YOUNG WOMAN: How clever you are! How good!

FAMOUS ACTRESS: I'm neither better nor worse than any other girl in the theater. Even though you do consider us such monsters.

EARNEST YOUNG WOMAN: *[Contritely.]* I have been a perfect fool.

FAMOUS ACTRESS: Well, you do look a bit silly, standing there with tears in your eyes, and your face flushed with happiness because you have discovered that a little blond man with spectacles loves you, after all. My dear, no man deserves to be adored as much as that. But then it's your own affair, isn't it?

EARNEST YOUNG WOMAN: Yes.

FAMOUS ACTRESS: Yet I want to give you a parting bit of advice: don't let him fool you like this again.

EARNEST YOUNG WOMAN: He won't. Never fear!

FAMOUS ACTRESS: No matter what you may find in his pockets--letters, handkerchiefs, my photograph, no matter what flowers he sends, or letters he writes, or appointments he makes--don't be taken in a second time.

EARNEST YOUNG WOMAN: You may be sure of that. And you won't say anything to him about my coming here, will you?

FAMOUS ACTRESS: Not a word. I'm angry with him for not having come to me frankly for permission to use my name the way he did.

EARNEST YOUNG WOMAN: You are a dear, and I don't know how to thank you.

FAMOUS ACTRESS: Now you mustn't begin crying all over again.

EARNEST YOUNG WOMAN: You have made me so happy!

[She kisses the FAMOUS ACTRESS impetuously, wetting her cheek with tears; then she rushes out. The door closes behind her. There is a pause.]

FAMOUS ACTRESS: *[Goes to the door of her boudoir, calls.]* All right, Alfred. You can come in now. She has gone.

CURTAIN

THE SEQUEL

Percival Wilde

CHARACTERS:

HE
SHE
THE BUTLER
HORROCKS, INC.

[The prologue may be spoken by any man who can wear full dress becomingly, generally The Butler.]

PROLOGUE: Do you recall the situation on which the curtain has fallen thousands of times in thousands of well-regulated dramas? Do you remember how they faced each other, and how there were tears in his eyes-- or her eyes--or their eyes? Do you mentally picture how he--or she--or they brushed the above-mentioned tears away? Or let them remain where they were? And how she whispered, "Yes, Jack" -- or "Yes, William" -- or "Yes, Eliphalet" -- as the case might have been? Or sometimes only plain "Yes?" And how he, with the expertness gained by many rehearsals, gathered her into his arms, and printed a kiss on her brow -- or her cheek -- or her hair -- or behind her ear -- but only in the rarest of instances on her lips? And how the happy pair, now forever united -- until the next performance -- stood looking out over the footlights, estimating the box-office receipts and the amount of paper in the house, until the curtain fell, and the thoughts of the audience turned to the inner man?

And then? What happens next? There are inquisitive souls who ask that question. Will they live happily ever afterward? Or will the matrimonial bark encounter one of the many obstacles which somehow have been forgotten? The dramatist, looking upon marriage, or its forerunner, engagement, as the end of all things, neglects to tell us. Starting with a variable number of eligible young persons of opposite sex, he has paired them off in such combinations as his experience tells him will be pleasing to the magnate who produces the play, to the temperamental ladies and gentlemen who condescend to act in it, and, last and most important, to that source from which all royalties flow, that unaccountable, irresponsible, conscienceless creature, the audience. To the very portals of marriage he travels with his charges, but there he leaves them, to act as guide, philosopher, friend to others following in their footsteps.

And then? Perhaps they do not live happily ever after. Perhaps she is extravagant, or he smokes in the parlor. Or he repents his rashness in recanting bachelorhood, and she reflects, as his faults become plain to her, that she might have done better. And they do not increase and multiply, and are unhappy, and so come to furnish material for another play.

But of the time between? Of the time immediately after she has said "Yes" and before she has begun to say "No?"

[The person who has spoken the prologue bows and retires. The curtain rises. It is early evening, and they are in the parlor of her house. There are heavy tapestries at the doors and perfectly opaque hangings at the windows--which is satisfactory, for even in the subdued light neither would welcome the inspection of a third person.]

HE: *[interrupting his embrace for an instant to hold her off at arms' length and look into her eyes]* Milly!

SHE: *[blushing prettily]* Jack!

[They embrace again.]

HE: *[after a pause]* So -- so you're going to marry me!

SHE: Yes, Jack. *[She looks up at him shyly.]* Isn't it wonderful? *[He nods.]* To think that we two--just we two---- *[He kisses her again. There is another pause.]* Come ... *[She draws him to a sofa.]*, we have so much to say to each other! Isn't that so?

[He is a little uneasy; even embarrassed. It is easy to see that sentiment is not his forte. On the other hand, she is absolutely at home. She has spent a considerable portion of her twenty-odd years looking forward to this moment. Now that it has come she is completely mistress of the situation. He seats himself on the sofa--a little gingerly--not that he is afraid of hurting the sofa, but because his entire attitude, now that the worst is over, has become distinctively timid; because some sixth sense warns him that he will not appear to his best advantage in the nonsensical half-hour which is to follow, and which by no possible device may be avoided. Once seated he recalls his duty sufficiently to put his arms round her in rather a clumsy fashion. She, however, is not satisfied, and releasing his clasp, rises with delicious abandon and installs herself on his lap. There is a further pause.]

HE: Are you comfortable--dear?

SHE: Perfectly! Perfectly! *[She closes her eyes contentedly. He, rather relieved that he no longer has to meet them, looks at her sharply. She is rather a winsome bit of femininity, whether he knows it or not. She puts her lips close to his ear.]* Jack!

HE: *[starting]* Yes? *[Correcting himself.]* Yes, dear?

SHE: Now that we are alone -- we are alone, aren't we?

HE: Of course.

[He looks round nervously.]

SHE: There is one thing I want you to tell me.

HE: Yes?

SHE: Jack, when did you begin to love me?

HE: *[flushing uncomfortably]* Well----

SHE: *[closing her eyes in anticipation]* Yes?

HE: When I began to love you?

SHE: Yes.

HE: *[plunging in]* Well, I think it was the first time I met you.

SHE: *[sitting bolt upright in surprise]* Jack! You don't mean it!

HE: I am quite sure. It was in December, a year ago.

SHE: *[surprised]* What?

HE: *[holding his ground]* Just after Christmas.

SHE: But that wasn't the first time I met you! It was long before that!

HE: Was it?

SHE: *[a little disappointed]* Didn't you know? It was at Barton's house party, Jack.

HE: Oh. *[After a pause, with a sickly smile.]* Barton's house party. So it was!

SHE: And then the second time-- *[Sinking back into his arms.]* When was it, Jack?

HE: The second time?

SHE: Yes.

HE: The time after Barton's?

SHE: Yes, Jack.

HE: *[thinking desperately, then turning on her suddenly]* Don't you know?

SHE: Of course I know. *[She sits up slowly.]* You don't mean to say you've forgotten that also?

HE: I'm sorry.

SHE: *[indignantly]* Sorry?

HE: I'm absent-minded, you know.

SHE: And you loved me from the first time we met! *[She rises in vexation.]* Oh! And I thought everything would be so different!

HE: *[also rising]* Now, Milly, don't get angry.

SHE: *[coming back to him]* I'm not angry, Jack. I'm hurt--just hurt.

HE: *[putting his arms round her]* I made a mistake, that's all. I thought the first time was later on.

SHE: In December?

HE: Yes.

SHE: Where?

HE: Eh?

SHE: Where did we meet in December, Jack? Just after Christmas?

HE: It's on the tip of my tongue.

SHE: *[waiting impatiently]* Well?

HE: *[triumphantly]* At Phelps'! It was at Phelps'! You see, I know, Milly! Am I right?

SHE: *[capitulating]* Yes, Jack.

HE: That was the time! Father was there too. You see, I remember! You made a hit with him. Coming home together he said, "Jack, that's an awfully nice young woman. I'd like you to know her better."

SHE: He said that about me?

HE: *[nodding emphatically]* Why, that wasn't a marker to the rest of the things he said!

SHE: Oh.

HE: You see *[with a vapid smile]*, Father's been wanting me to get married off for years.

SHE: *[horrified]* Oh!

HE: *[stopping as if shot]* I haven't said anything wrong, have I?

SHE: Wrong? No. Oh, no! *[She smiles with an effort.]* Go on, Jack.

HE: *[suspicious]* Look here! I'm not offending you--

SHE: *[interrupting]* Offending? We haven't been engaged an hour?

HE: *[not entirely reassured]* Father told me to be careful what I said tonight.

SHE: With your future wife, Jack? Careful?

HE: *[nodding soberly]* He said that if I was in any doubt I should talk about him.

SHE: Oh! *[She smiles sweetly.]* Go on, Jack.

HE: What?

SHE: Talk about him.

HE: *[after an irresolute pause]* Well, father's a great man. You know that.

SHE: Everybody knows it, Jack.

HE: Of course! Father owns the biggest department store in town. Why, he started the department-store idea! There were no department stores before father.

SHE: *[lackadaisically]* How intensely thrilling!

HE: His first store--have you ever seen a picture of it?

SHE: No.

HE: It wasn't as large as this room. And today there are more than three thousand people working for Horrocks, Incorporated! *[He pauses. She waits for him to continue.]* Father has to have someone to carry on the business after him, and it would break his heart to have it go out of the family. He wants me to grow into his boots.

SHE: *[settling herself comfortably; not, however, on his lap]* And is that why he wanted you to be married?

HE: *[smiling]* Indirectly, yes.

SHE: I don't understand, Jack.

HE: You see, a man's so much steadier when he's got a wife.

SHE: *[thoughtfully]* Y-e-s.

[There is a pause.]

HE: Well, I have to be going.

[He rises.]

SHE: Already?

HE: Father'll be waiting.

SHE: *[looking at him in open-eyed astonishment]* What do you mean?

HE: He'll want to know what happened.

SHE: *[trying to grasp the idea]* What happened?

HE: Whether you said yes or no.

SHE: *[with sudden comprehension]* Oh! So he knew you were going to ask me?

HE: Of course!

SHE: You told him?

HE: *[hesitantly]* W-e-e-ll----

SHE: *[furiously]* You had the aud-- *[with hardly a break she continues in the most honeyed tones]* or perhaps he told you? *[Delilahlike she throws her arms about his neck.]* Come, 'fess up!

HE: *[with a broad smile]* Well, he said: "If you haven't asked her before morning--" *[He pauses.]*

SHE: *[encouragingly]* Yes?

HE: *[laughing]* He said, "--you can go to work for ten dollars a week."

SHE: So--you asked her?

HE: *[with a guffaw]* Well, what do you think?

SHE: And you knew she'd accept?

HE: *[chuckling]* We-ell--

SHE: *[mimicking him]* We-ell--

HE: I wasn't sure.

SHE: No?

HE: But father was!

SHE: *[flinging him off]* You little beast!

HE: *[surprised]* Milly! Now I haven't offended you again, have I?

SHE: Offended me! Ha!

HE: It's only my way of talking. I don't mean anything by it--

SHE: *[interrupting]* No; I didn't think so.

[She flounces off to the end of the room.]

HE: Now, Milly!

[There is a pause. Then she returns, with her feelings under control again.]

SHE: I was only fooling, Jack. Tell me more about it.

HE: Not if you're so touchy, Milly.

SHE: Touchy? No. I'm just a little excited, that's all. Don't you think any girl would be if she knew she was going to marry the son of Horrocks, Incorporated?

HE: *[after an uncertain pause]* Father's waiting for me.

SHE: Let him wait. It's only ten.

HE: *[shaking his head vigorously]* Father likes to get to bed early. You see, he's always at the store when it opens; makes it a point to be the first one down.

SHE: But tonight, Jack--he won't mind staying up a little later tonight. *[As he dissents.]* You have only a block to go.

HE: *[hesitantly]* I don't know. Father said--

SHE: *[interrupting]* We'll write him a note, Jack.

HE: A note?

SHE: Explain matters. I'll send it round with the butler.

HE: Father mightn't like it.

SHE: He'll have to give in to me this once! *[She has already seated herself at a writing table.]* He'll be up, won't he?

HE: *[gloomily]* You bet he will! At any rate, till I get home.

SHE: Ring the bell for Robert.

[He does so, and remains at the door watching her.]

HE: What are you writing?

SHE: *[rising with the note and folding it]* Finished already!

HE: It can't be very long.

SHE: It doesn't have to be--dear.

[She slips the note into its envelope.]

THE BUTLER: *[appearing in the doorway]* Yes, miss?

SHE: *[handing him the note]* Take this right over to Mr. Horrocks. Take it over yourself.

THE BUTLER: Yes, miss. Any answer?

SHE: No. Just give it to Mr. Horrocks himself. And hurry, Robert.

[The butler goes.]

HE: *[uneasily]* I don't know how he'll like it.

SHE: Leave it to me, Jack. Come, sit down. *[She puts her hand over his lips as he tries to speak.]* Just think; all the questions I'm dying to ask you!

HE: Questions? What questions?

SHE: You're not afraid to answer me, are you?

HE: *[with a dismal attempt at humor]* I thought that didn't come till you were married.

SHE: That's still some distance away, Jack. *[She looks at him keenly.]* You're twenty-six, aren't you? *[He nods.]* And your father's been anxious to have you married?

HE: Ever since I left college.

SHE: Oh. *[She pauses an instant; then, making a shrewd guess.]* Jack, what is her name?

HE: What do you mean?

SHE: You know what I mean.

HE: *[slowly comprehending, shocked]* Milly! That's nothing for you!

SHE: But I'm engaged, Jack. And engaged girls can discuss all kinds of subjects. *[As he shakes his head.]* But they do! Particularly with their fiancés. *[He is unconvinced.]* Jack, if we can't have full confidence in each other now-- *[She breaks off.]*

HE: *[after a pause]* Who told you?

SHE: *[concealing her triumph]* That's not a fair question.

HE: Why not?

SHE: Oh, the things that girls talk about-- *[She waves her hand vaguely.]*

HE: *[interested]* Yes?

SHE: *[with a happy inspiration]* The things that married men tell their wives--

HE: Oh.

SHE: And the wives tell their sisters, and the sisters tell their best friends, and the best friends tell everybody else. Women can't keep secrets--you know that.

HE: Yes.

SHE: *[after a judicious pause, quite casually]* What show is she with now, Jack?

HE: *[thoughtlessly]* She's not working just now.

[Suddenly recollecting, he bends a suspicious glance on her, but her expression is innocence itself.]

SHE: *[addressing her remarks to the ceiling]* Such a pity! *[She pauses; he is still watching her.]* She has talent; there's no doubt of that.

HE: How do you know that if you don't know her name?

SHE: *[bluffing desperately]* Why, I've seen her!

HE: *[incredulously]* Seen her?

SHE: *[meeting his glance naïvely]* She was the fourth from the right, wasn't she?

HE: No; the second. *[Still uneasy, he pauses again.]*

SHE: You see, I know.

HE: And you don't feel differently toward me on account of it?

SHE: *[laughing]* Differently? How absurd, Jack! I never thought you were an angel.

HE: *[quite reassured]* She's a lady--a real lady--much too good for that sort of thing.

SHE: I could see that from where I was sitting.

HE: Her real name's Eliza, but she calls herself Corinne.

SHE: I don't blame her. Corinne is a pretty name. *[With a covert look at him.]* And she's just as good-hearted as she's beautiful, isn't she, Jack?

HE: How did you know?

SHE: *[proceeding fluently]* She has talent--real talent--only they haven't recognized it yet. But they're going to some day! All she needs is a chance to make good! And you're going to see that she gets it, aren't you, Jack?

HE: *[enthusiastically]* You bet I am!

SHE: *[nodding sagely]* She's been unfortunate, but she's a lady through it all. And no affectation, no airs about her. She's an awfully good little sport-- a real pal! Only your father can't see it that way.

HE: *[astonished]* Did he tell you about her?

SHE: *[without answering]* That was why he was so anxious to get you married. He wanted you safe--away from her.

HE: You knew all along?

SHE: And never let on!

HE: *[delightedly]* Well! Well! I can hardly believe it!

SHE: I wanted you to tell me.

HE: *[with real enthusiasm]* Say, we're going to get along!

SHE: Aren't we though?

HE: Milly, you're a good little sport yourself!

SHE: Do you really think so?

HE: I never would have believed it of you!

SHE: Thanks. Thanks, Jack. And do you want to know something else? I'm not even going to make you give her up.

HE: *[astonished]* What?

SHE: Spoil a beautiful friendship? No, Jack. I'm not like your father. I know what it means to you. I appreciate such things.

HE: Milly!

SHE: Are you shocked?

HE: Do you mean it? Do you honestly mean it?

[She tries to answer, but it is too much for her sense of humor. She bursts into almost hysterical laughter.]

HE: *[rising anxiously]* Milly!

SHE: *[between spasms]* You don't understand me, do you, Jack? But your father will! You can be sure of that! *[He watches her in absolute mystification.]* Because he's coming here, Jack! I am expecting him at any moment.

HE: *[thunderstruck]* Coming here? Is that what you wrote? You didn't have the nerve!

SHE: But I did, Jack!

HE: You shouldn't have done it! He'll be angry. Good Lord, he'll be angry! He never goes out at this time of night! Hasn't for years!

SHE: Listen!

[Footsteps--hurried footsteps--are heard ascending the stairs, and THE BUTLER, not the sedate, punctilious butler of a few minutes ago, but a

panting, very much frightened butler, who has not even paused to remove his hat and coat, stands in the doorway.]

THE BUTLER: *[announcing hastily]* Mr. Horrocks!

[There is a rush. The Butler is swept aside and Horrocks, Inc., stands in his place. And Horrocks, Inc., is angry, angry with capital letters, angrier than either he or anybody else has been before. The small eyes of the department-store genius dart lightning, his hands tremble, his lips move, but no words known to the English language issue from them. Yet he is a mass of sounds-- explosive sounds, sibilant sounds, rumbling sounds; such sounds as might come from a small volcano immediately before the eruption; such sounds as might result were an intoxicated Zulu, holding a spoonful of hot mush in his mouth the while, to attempt a Russian folk-song set to music by Claude Debussy. Were an artist present he might ask Horrocks, Inc., to pose as the God of Anger. And, most disrespectfully, Milly continues to laugh, still more hysterically than ever.]

HE: *[petrified with terror]* Father!

[Horrocks, Inc., rushes at him as if he would brain him. But the clenched fist stops under the young man's nose, and, for the first time, one notices that it brandishes a crumpled sheet of paper.]

HE: *[taking it, panic-stricken]* Wh-what she wrote you?

[Horrocks, Inc., assents with frightful noises.]

HE: *[backing away]* May I read it?

[Horrocks, Inc., assents as before. More than that, his terrific gestures indicate that he emphatically desires the young man to read it--to read it aloud.]

HE: *[still retreating from the impending destruction]* "Dear Mister Department Store----" *[With incredulous appeal.]* You wrote that, Milly?

HORROCKS, INC: *[at length forming intelligible words]* Go on! Go on!

HE: "Please call for goods to be returned."

[Horror-stricken, he turns to the spot where, an instant ago, Milly was standing. But she has vanished. The Butler, too, has fled. And squarely between himself and the door stands the fearful figure of Horrocks, Inc.]

CURTAIN

MORE BOOKS FROM BLACK BOX PRESS

* * *

Three Plays of the Absurd – by Walter Wykes
Ten 10-Minute Plays – edited by Walter Wykes

Printed in November 2021
by Rotomail Italia S.p.A., Vignate (MI) - Italy